Gift of the Desert Dog

Robert L. Hunton

Open Books
PRESS

Published by Open Books Press, USA
www.openbookspress.com

An imprint of Pen & Publish, Inc.
Bloomington, Indiana
(812) 837-9226
info@PenandPublish.com

www.PenandPublish.com

ISBN: 978-0-9845751-8-3
Library of Congress Control Number: 2010940074

This book is printed on acid free paper.

Printed in the USA

For Julie,
her faith in me is undying

Acknowledgments

The author wishes to express thanks to the Tohono O'odham Nation of southern Arizona and Sonoran Mexico, whose consideration, patience, and guidance helped make this story possible. The symbols used in *Gift of the Desert Dog* are O'odham property and are being used by permission.

Particular gratitude is expressed to the members of the O'odham Cultural Preservation Committee of the Tohono O'odham Tribal Council, Sells, Arizona; Frances Conde, chairperson, Timothy Joaquim, Wavalene Saunders, Felicia Nuñez, and Frances Miguel. Also, Dena Thomas, librarian, Venito Garcia Library, Sells, Arizona, for her kind cooperation and extensive knowledge.

Special appreciation is extended to Dr. James S. Griffith, formerly of the University of Arizona's Southwest Folklore Center, for his introductions in the Tohono O'odham community.

A personal debt of gratitude is owed to fellow teacher and Vermont author, Jim DeFilippi, whose encouragement and support has meant so much; to Arizona children's author, Jennifer J. Stewart, for her thoughtfulness and talented insight; to my agent, Andrew Whelchel, for believing in me and this story; and to the students and faculty of Colchester, Vermont Middle School, particularly, Angelika Mahoney, school librarian, for their support and patience, waiting for my stories to see print.

Key to the Illustrations

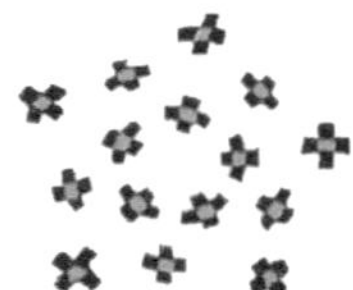

Coyote tracks (imagine a dog's footprint in the sand ❈ . Coyote is both the great one and the foolish one; he is cunning and unpredictable, but also a survivor.)

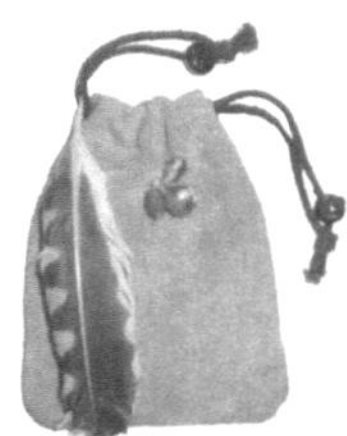

Antelope skin medicine pouch (among the sacred items found in Jonathan Gray Horse's power collection are quartz crystals, owl feather, claw of a sharp-shinned hawk, Santa Cruz stone)

Cross or four directions (think of the compass pointing north, south, east, and west; symbolic of journeys taken)

Man-in-the-maze (imagine a creation story; the first human being born from Mother Earth. Also signifies life's cycles, eternal motion, and the choices we must make)

Table of Contents

*From desert dust and blown
among prickly shadows comes
this old man coyote*

~ O'odham legend ~

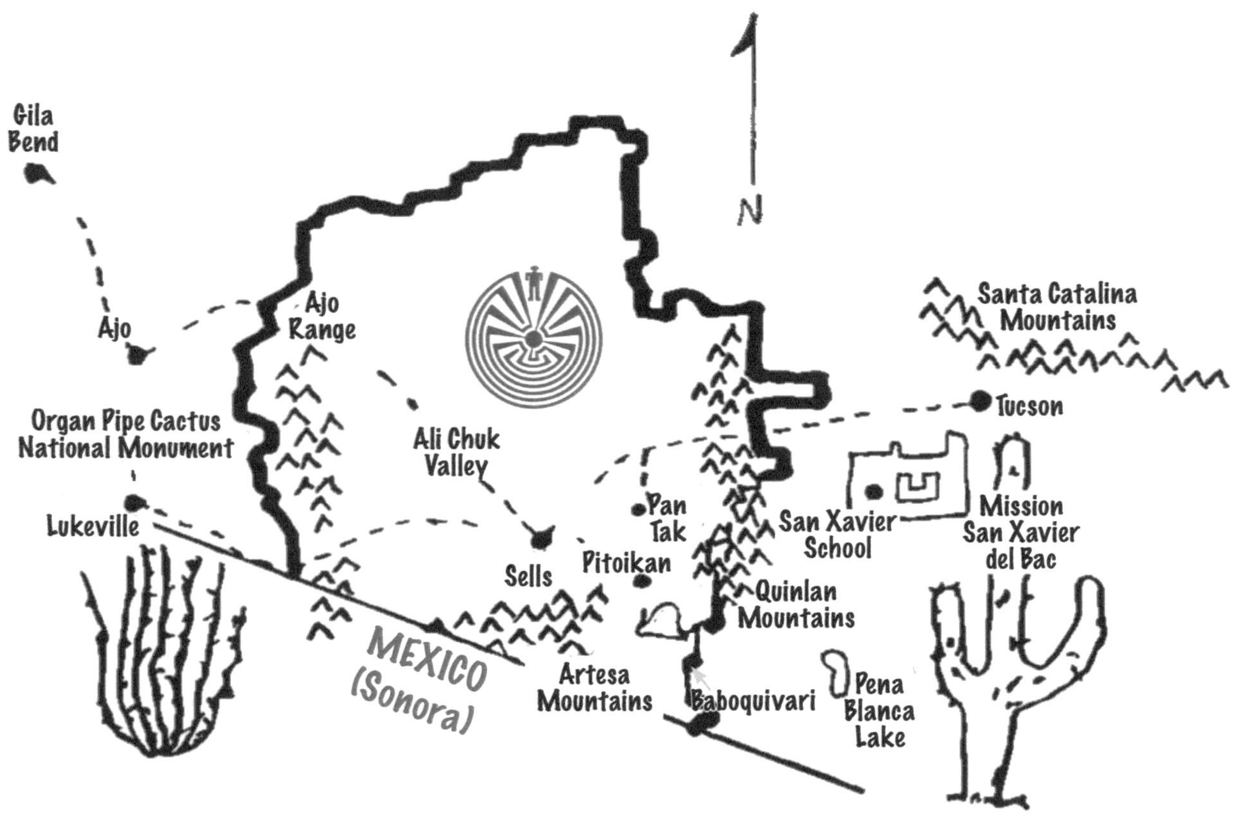

The Borderlands
Gila Bend
N
Ajo
Ajo Range
Santa Catalina Mountains
Organ Pipe Cactus National Monument
Tucson
Ali Chuk Valley
Lukeville
Pan Tak
San Xavier School
Mission San Xavier del Bac
Sells
Pitoikan
MEXICO (Sonora)
Quinlan Mountains
Artesa Mountains
Baboquivari
Pena Blanca Lake

Part One

Danny's Trial

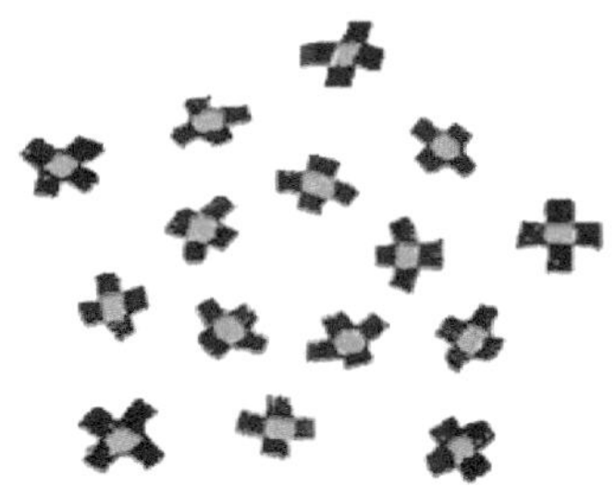

1

"So, little yellow and orange—little nippy one, have you been crawling on a rainbow?"

Danny Rivas spied the beautifully beaded lizard sunning itself on a boulder. The creature curled defensively, flicking its tongue between warning hisses.

"Cut the squawking, I'm not going to hurt you," he said, carefully reaching toward its head with a stick. "Besides, you're the one with all the poison. Yeah, I know about you, you're a snapping turtle without its shell. Hey, are you listening...?"

The animal quietly focused on the end of the shaft.

"...Because if you are, you're the only one. Nobody listens to me—ever, except maybe Digs—and Grandfather." He sighed deeply. "That's the trouble with all of them. They don't care about me. And why should they? I'm just a dumb little punk, anyway."

Again the lizard hissed and snapped in his direction.

"Okay, okay, I'll mind my own business," he muttered, "but do me a favor, will you? The next time you see my father...or those pinheads at school, bite them, and tell them Danny sent you. Maybe that will wake them up, got it?"

Heavy rain clouds in the mountains and a rushing sound behind him went unheeded. He tossed the stick aside as the lizard lumbered into the safety of a crevice.

And then, suddenly engulfed in a torrent, he was swept away by a muddy wall of water, coughing and choking as he swallowed the flow into his lungs. Bobbing branches struck his head and uprooted prickly pear speared his arms. He lunged at the bank of the wash, but a jutting snag of mesquite roots passed just beyond his fingertips. He gulped air as he rolled, flailing his arms to keep his face above water. Beneath the surface, rocks and thorny ocotillo scraped and tore at his flesh.

He quickly became disoriented in the swirling, boiling tidal wave. It took all of his strength to stay upright, fighting the sandy bottom with his legs. He gritted his teeth, loudly cursing his carelessness.

"Gila monster, you didn't warn me," he gasped.

Down the channel he plunged, growing steadily weaker from the pounding of the rocks and debris against his body. Casting a frightened eye at the steep side of the wash, he tried desperately to move toward it, but he was caught in a jam of brush as the powerful current pulled him back into midstream.

"Grandfather, I forgot. I'm sorry..."

It was then he realized that nature's fury would not release him; no matter how hard he struggled, and he began to let go. Gray shadows clouded his eyes and a buzzing sound increased to a shrill ringing in his ears. He let his body relax, to drift and float freely.

"Is this what it feels like, Grandfather..." he asked from the edge of a dream, "...to make the final journey?" But there was no answer, only the faraway sound of rushing water.

His chest slammed the fallen sycamore with tremendous force, knocking the air from his lungs. In desperation, he threw his arms across one side of the massive trunk. There he clung precariously, gasping for breath, as the cold down current threatened to pull him under again. The muscles in his arms burned from the strain, yet he managed to hold on.

"P-Please—I can't..." he mumbled, gazing weakly at sky spirits overhead.

The surge lifted him and he lost his grip. Caught in a giant funnel, he was sucked beneath the tree. Breaking the surface, he crashed heavily into a tangle of dead branches. A firm hold on an overhanging limb kept his head above water, but his leg was wedged tightly below the surface. He was trapped in the flow, unable to break free, while the litter from the wash continued to batter him. Without hope and exhausted from the struggle, he lowered his head and cried.

The growling came from directly behind—low at first, then a snarl. He turned sharply toward the sound, unsure of how close. Wiping tears and muddy grime from his face, he tried to focus his eyes on a dark form just above him. There, in the twisted wreckage of the sycamore, was a dog. It was a very large dog with a long nose and a dusky brown coat. Danny shifted his weight to get a better look. It bared its teeth, shying back slightly.

You are not a dog, he thought. *You're too big—and your teeth are too sharp.*

He could see that it was trapped, as he was, but not in the same way. The animal's legs were free, while tightly cinched around its upper torso was a thick nylon rope. The long ragged end of the cord was wrapped in a maze of branches close to Danny's arm.

"It's a snare. Old Coyote, you've been here for a while, haven't you?"

The wild dog pulled on the line, whining and snarling. As it continued to resist, the rope became ever tighter around its body.

Danny studied the end of the cord. By reaching up and untangling the knotted mess, he could release the coyote. And he saw a chance for himself.

If I hold on tightly, you will try to pull away. Are you strong enough to free my leg?

It was a slow and difficult task unraveling the wet strand with one hand, while he held himself up with the other. As he worked, he carefully wound the cord around his wrist. At last he was ready to release his unsuspecting ally. He pulled repeatedly on the line, watching the coyote intently.

With a yelp and a gnarl, the animal yanked back on the cord. It began to backpedal, digging its paws into the rough bark and biting at the noose around its body.

"Please, Coyote, don't bite through the line!"

Slowly he felt the pressure release around his leg. It was working! He closed his eyes in silent prayer as the creature tugged and jerked on the rope. Inch by inch, Danny's body was dragged from the water. With a final push of his feet, he escaped the current and crawled cautiously up the branch.

The dog was not yet free and continued its desperate tugging and growling. Each time it felt pressure it yanked even harder.

Danny felt his hand grow numb as the wrist cord tightened, cutting off circulation. Glancing at the animal, he saw that the rope had hiked up its body, allowing it to apply more tension on the line. He tried twisting his wrist to unwind the cord and release his hold.

With a sudden snap the cinch broke from around the dog's body, freeing it from the deadly snare. It whirled about in confusion, nipping at imaginary threats. Gradually it calmed and began to move slowly back along the trunk of the tree. It watched him as it went, the foam of frantic struggle dripping from its mouth.

And then, the wild dog's nose caught the wind. And it was as if Danny were no longer there—invisible. It lifted its head, gazing off into the distance. For a brief moment it stood listening, and then turned silently, disappearing over the bank into thick shadows of mesquite.

He lay exhausted among the limbs, his bruised and bleeding body shivering with cold. But he was alive, and thankful the animal had chosen not to attack him, for he hadn't the strength to defend himself.

A vision of the tiny ranch house where he lived on the San Xavier reservation south of Tucson, Arizona flashed before his eyes. He could see his sister, Sophie, sitting on the front step laughing with her girlfriend. The old white Ranchero parked in the dirt driveway belonged to Amelia Simpson, a neighbor from Pan Tak. She was always there the first of each month to have her hair trimmed in his mother, Cecilia's, makeshift style salon. His father, Tony, had left early in the pickup, probably to haul gravel to that landscaping job in the city. Everything seemed normal around the yard, except that he, Danny Rivas, was nowhere to be found. Did anyone care? And there was his friend, Digs (he could call him that, but he was Diego to those at school), standing out by the gate, searching the terrain with his eyes.

"Digs, I'm here," he sputtered. "You won't believe it—a coyote..."

Who would believe his tale of deliverance? He closed his eyes to the water rushing below him and slept.

"Sophie, someone's knocking. Get that, will you?" Cecilia shouted from the kitchen as she wrapped the woman's hair in a towel. The rapping on the door came louder. "Uh, where is she? Sophie...Excuse me, Amelia, I'll be right back." Shaking her head, she padded away in slippered feet.

"I told him Danny wasn't home, Momma," Sophie announced from beyond the screen. She wrinkled her nose at Diego Ramirez, who stood awkwardly by. "See? You should always listen to girls. We don't lie."

"Hello Digs. Yes, this time she *is* right," chided Cecilia, giving her wide-eyed daughter the stare. "Danny left maybe two hours ago. I don't know, he was angry again about something—wouldn't talk about it—just took off. It looked to me like he was headed for Little Wild Horse Canyon." She pointed at the rugged hillside rising above the desert green. "It's been raining up there most of the morning, and I sure don't like it. It's lunchtime and his stomach usually wins out over his head. I'm sorry, Digs, are you hungry?"

"No, that's okay, Mrs. Rivas, I'll go to meet him."

"Not a bad idea," she nodded, casting a worried look at the dark thunderclouds above Helmet Peak. "There'll be some of my fry bread waiting—when you two get back."

"No problem, Mrs. Rivas, no problem..."

2

Whit...whit...whit...wheeeeet.

A thrasher bird sounded from a nearby cholla. Its sickle-like beak made the perfect siphon as it probed the thorns for nectar.

The late afternoon sun warmed Danny's cheeks and glowed through his eyelids. He forced them open as the wind whipped a leafy twig against his face. Lifting his head slowly, he gazed along the litter-strewn wash, now windswept and dry.

"Ooooh, my arm."

Gently, he flexed his shoulder muscle—it was stiff and sore. Beneath him a sharp branch jabbed his ribs and his legs ached painfully. He rolled off the limb, landing with a thump in the sand. His head throbbed from a large welt above his temple.

Pressing it gingerly, he winced as a dagger of pain shot across his forehead and into his cheekbone.

"This is no dream, it hurts too much," he groaned, peering through torn jeans at a deep gash in his knee. Dried blood had caked around the wound, sticking it to his pant leg. He tried to peel it away, but his hands shook and it tore loose.

"Aaaah...God."

He grit his teeth, his body stiffened. For several more minutes, he tried to lay still and listen to his lungs taking in air. Slowly, carefully, he flexed other parts of his body, checking for injury. But in spite of his rough tumble down the wash, nothing seemed broken. He was scraped and cut, his T-shirt was in rags, and the legs of his jeans were nearly torn off at the knees. Add to this a missing sneaker, and he was in no shape to make the hike back down the steep ravine.

It was then he heard a familiar call from the far end of the wash. Grasping the branch above his head, he pulled himself into a sitting position. Expelling air through clenched teeth, he hoisted his beaten body up onto one leg. Limping out into the open, away from the tangle of branches, he eased himself onto a rock to watch the figure of his friend approaching.

"Hey, what's up?" yelled Digs, carefully picking his way up the streambed. "Whoa, Man, you don't look so good. What happened?" he asked, finally coming to a halt beside Danny's battered form.

"A little accident, that's all. I'll be fine."

"You look like a mountain lion beat you up."

"Are you kidding? I sure wouldn't be talking to you now."

"So, okay, a javelina then."

"Come on, Digs, I..."

"Sorry, I don't think I'd be laughing either if I looked like you do."

"It's pretty bad, huh?" He took another look at the damage. "It was this wicked flood—came out of nowhere. Wait 'til Mom sees me."

"Your mom, what about your father?"

"Huh, yeah, it'll just give him another reason to yell at me. Without a doubt, it'll be a lecture from both of them."

"Why? Because you're an Indian and you should know better than to get caught in a wash?"

"Hey, shut up, lame brain."

"Sorry, Danny, that's not what I meant..."

"Sure it was. You think I'm dumb too, don't you?" He pushed on Digs' chest. "Well, how does this sound, genius. I was saved by a coyote."

"You were...Come on, that's not possible."

"I'm serious, Digs. It was trapped in that tree...had a snare wrapped around itself. It must have traveled quite a distance before getting snagged. I'll bet it came from off the reservation. No O'odham would do that to Coyote. Anyhow, we sort of took care of each other's problem."

"A coyote? We'd better keep this between you and me," he advised, "if you know what I mean."

"Well, you're the dumb one, because a smart person would know that coyotes do amazing things. Ask my grandfather if you don't believe me. He'll tell you."

"Okay, so say it's true. Will it matter when you get home?"

Danny stared at the cut on his knee. "I-I guess you're..."

"Yeah, I'm right," Digs declared. "And here's another thing... don't let the guys at school find out about this, especially Jake and Eddie."

"You've got that right," Danny sighed.

"Okay, come on, give me your arm, we've got to get back. Your mom looked a little worried."

"Was Sophie there when you left?"

"Yeah, with her friend, Shawna."

"Just great, they'll tell the whole world."

"Tell the world what?" asked Digs. "They don't need to know about the coyote."

"Promise me, you won't..."

"My lips are sealed, amigo."

Cecilia watched through the screen as Amelia's Ranchero disappeared down the road in a cloud of dust, but she was no longer thinking of her most loyal customer.

"Danny's never this late," she fretted. "Sophie, come in now and help me in the kitchen. I've got to prepare more food for when they get here. Shawna, we've eaten, but would you like something?"

"Okay, Mrs. Rivas. Are you sure there's enough?"

"Of course...Ooops, I forgot about Digs, he loves my refried."

"Does he have to stay, Momma?"

"Sophie, your manners, please."

"He always looks at me cross-eyed. I think there's something wrong with him," she announced, watching a grin break on Shawna's face.

"Well, he's Danny's friend—and that's quite enough," Cecilia replied, rolling out bread dough made earlier and stored in their small icebox.

"Daddy doesn't like him," Sophie added.

"Sophie, how do you know that? And listen, your father works very long hours. I'd appreciate it if you left him out of this, okay?"

"I'm serious, he doesn't. He gets mad at Danny for goofing off all the time when he's around Digs."

"You let us worry about Danny's goofing. And speaking of... Where are they? Shawna honey, could I ask you to keep an eye out by the front door?"

A sudden tapping at the kitchen doorjamb had them spinning about. There stood Digs Ramirez, peering into the light of the room. Behind him waited Danny, carefully watching over his friend's shoulder for the expression on Cecilia's face.

"Hello, Mrs. Rivas, a-are you cooking beans for the fry bread?"

"Oh, thank God, you made it. Yes, Digs, how could I disappoint you?" She stretched to see her son. "Danny, where have you been hiding? You've...Danny Rivas?!" She stared at his tattered appearance. "Wha...what has happened? Look at you."

"Mom, please, I..."

"No please." She moved quickly to his side. "Your arms—and your leg. Tell me now, what happened to you?"

"I-It was raining in the mountains." He looked quickly at Digs. "I fell in the wash."

"That's right, Mrs. Rivas, t-the bank gave way," Digs lied.

"Digs, I will speak with my son."

"Sorry, I'll just go and sit over here..."

"And where is your sneaker? All right, now out with it," she demanded, "the truth this time."

"That is the truth," he cried. "Why is it you don't believe me? You never believe me."

"Yeah, you mean like last week when you told Momma you were at Digs' house after school," Sophie injected, "when you really had a detention with Mr. Jensen?"

"Just shut up, Sophie, this is none of your business."

"Danny, don't talk to your sister that way. Now, I suggest you start again...or practice your story like crazy before your father gets home tonight."

"I don't care about a dumb story—and I don't care about him, either."

"You don't mean that," Cecilia frowned. "What has gotten into you?"

"What's gotten into me...is this place and all of you," he shouted. "It's always the same thing, gang up on Danny. Well, not anymore. Come on, Digs, let's get out of here."

"I think I h-have to go home now," stammered his friend.

"Sure, that's right, you too," choked Danny. "Okay, go." Turning quickly, he hobbled from the kitchen and out the front door.

Cecilia hurried after him. "Danny, don't. Where are you going?"

"Somewhere, anywhere...Who cares?!" he yelled, dragging himself stiffly across the yard.

She caught a final glimpse of his head and shoulders as he disappeared into the dense green of the Sonoran desert.

3

"Let him go, Momma. He's done this before and he always comes home," assured Sophie.

"Yes, and no thanks to you this time," Cecilia answered. "Your comment about Danny at school was unnecessary. You know how sensitive he's been lately."

"Gee, sorry...but he will come home, I said."

"Well, sorry isn't good enough. I should send you out there to find him."

"Huh, you can forget that," she pouted. "Shawna and I are going to her house this afternoon. Her mom's taking us to Target in Tucson." The girls exchanged quick looks.

"Tar...so, you have money to burn, do you? And shopping is more important than your brother?"

"This is not serious. Please, Momma..."

"All right, now let me tell you what will really happen today," she declared. "You will begin by heading back to the kitchen to finish preparing the food I had started. Shawna may help you, if she wishes." She swiped her hand across her brow, trying to wipe away the nervousness. "Shawna and Digs, this is not a reflection on either of you. You are always welcome, no matter what."

"I should go..." whispered Digs.

Cecilia didn't seem to hear. "After they've eaten, Sophie, you will work on your project for Indian Day at school. You need to have that ready by the end of the week, don't you? What about you, Shawna? You're in that class..."

"Um, yes, Mrs. Rivas, but I'm finished," she replied, wincing at Sophie.

"Oooo-kay, well, another exciting day in my boring life," Sophie muttered. "Come on, Shawna."

"Ayee, why does the world come apart so easily around here?" Cecilia cried after them.

Digs Ramirez slipped quietly past and headed down the steps to leave. He glanced back nervously.

"I'd better get going. I'm sorry, Mrs. Rivas..."

"Digs, please, sit with me on the steps a moment," she asked, plopping down wearily. "Do you have any idea where Danny might have gone?"

"Not really, uh, well, maybe to the shelter."

"What shelter?"

"The one made of ocotillo and grasses that he and his grandfather started in the fall—which we finished just a few weeks ago."

"Oh, yes, I think I remember Joseph mentioning it."

"It's over that way," he gestured loosely, "near Sheep's Head Rock—maybe two miles."

"What do you think?"

"He might be there..."

"Digs, I know it's out of your way, but would you?"

He worked the loose gravel with his toe. "Sure, I could."

"I'm sorry," she breathed, "I know you're not Danny's keeper and I won't ask again. It's just that if he's not back before Tony gets home...I don't know what might happen."

"Okay, Mrs. Rivas."

She hugged him tightly. "Wait, before you leave, take some of my fry bread and beans."

He collapsed out of breath in the dim shadows of the kih, or traditional house. This was what the O'odham called them; built with care from all that the desert could provide. Slender stems of ocotillo, lashed together and interwoven with mesquite branches, were topped with thick grass bundles. Much effort and patience were needed to create a single round room. Many kihs in reservation villages featured adobe ovens and attached ramadas. A ramada was a shaded area which cooled the entrance to the dwelling.

Danny and Joseph had slept under their ramada one warm evening to catch the desert breezes. He loved being with his grandfather at the kih. It was a place where he felt safe from the eyes of the world—safe to try to work things out in his mind. But he was still too angry to use his head wisely. He wiped sweat from his face with his tattered shirt. The gash in his knee ached and pain continued to shoot from his temple.

"They're so stupid...They don't understand me at all," he mumbled, "especially, him. To him, it's work, work, and more work. And when he's home, it's not to listen—like, ask me how things went at school or if I want to hang out or something— He'd rather go cruising with his friends and drink beer. Bah!" He swung his fist at the inside wall. "Ouch! Oooh, so is it my fault ocotillos have thorns?"

He breathed deeply, sucking at the puncture wound in his hand. A tiny droplet of blood appeared just above the welt in his wrist where the snare cord had been wrapped.

"And Sophie...man, is she ever dumb. That mouth of hers— she needs to put a sock in it. She walks around the house, so important and all, such a big shot in high school. Why doesn't Mom put her in her place? There's no way Coyote would save *her* life."

He rose slowly and walked in a circle around the fire pit. A blackened mesquite log lay among the charcoals where he and Digs had made camp three weeks before.

"I'll show them. I'll hide out here a while—make them worry. I'll skip school, too. They're all smiley when I get good grades. Let's see how they like a no-show." He ran his hand across his mouth. "I can sneak food in the neighborhood. I'll make a throwing spear like the one Grandfather made and hunt for a cottontail. And Digs will bring me food..."

Stepping out under the ramada, he watched the trail as it wound down from Sheep's Head Rock. Overhead, a pair of turkey vultures drifted effortlessly on warm currents of air. The sound of the wind rushing among the forest of giant saguaros created a natural rhythm in his ears, but it did little to soothe his anger.

"...except that he was acting like a jerk. I wonder what's eating him."

Satisfied that he had not been followed, Danny reentered the kih to fetch a large basket olla. The finely crafted container was stored along with two clay pots on a mat in the back of the room. The olla had been woven of tightly coiled yucca and made an excellent vessel in which to carry water. Rolled up inside one of the pots was a soft antelope skin. He would bring both to the spring down in the rocks where he would drink, wash himself, and clean out the cut in his knee.

"After a few days, they'll think I'm dead...and won't they be sorry then," he grumbled.

Arriving at the natural basin hidden in the shadows of a rock overhang, he lowered his body into the cold clear water. Closing his eyes, he gently rolled his neck and flexed his shoulders. The icy bath began to work miracles on his body and soul. Slowly, he let his muscles relax as the angry thoughts began to fade. In the cool quiet, a vision of his brush with death in the wash returned.

"Coyote, our meeting was strange, wasn't it? Grandfather told me the moon is your mother, but you found me under the sun. He was right though, you always have a plan for escaping the flood."

Smoothing the sand at the edge of the pool, he pushed the tip of his thumb into the soft surface four times; each dimple opposite the other to form a circular print. He made several more of the impressions in a gradual arc.

"There, coyote tracks."

He raised his upper body out of the stone basin and onto the ground while his legs remained submerged. With spring water brimming in the olla, he used the antelope skin and a chunk of soap tree yucca he had cut with his jackknife to cleanse the gash in his knee. The milky mixture soothed the stinging almost at once.

"Maybe I should...Yeah, the wash. There's no reason to keep this quiet. I'll make them all take notice of Danny Rivas." His eyes narrowed. "If I tell them how Coyote rescued me—announce it to everyone—I'll be important. Grandfather says a person who has met an animal is honored and takes the name deer-meeter or fox-meeter...so, I am coyote-meeter."

"Danny Rivas..." The call echoed off the cliff face and across the valley floor. "You're here...I know it. Come out, so we can talk."

"Digs...?" He turned from the sanctuary, staring into the afternoon sun. Gathering his belongings, he climbed with some effort over the rocks to a narrow footpath that led back to the kih. As he approached his friend from behind, he noticed him gazing at the far horizon. "Well, what do you want?"

"Ho! Man, you scared me," cried Digs with a jump.

"If you knew I was here, why are you scared?" Danny responded haughtily.

"Come on, lay off. What was I supposed to say in front of your family?"

"Nothing, that's the point. You were just supposed to come with me," he huffed. "I thought you were my friend."

"I am...I'm here now, aren't I?"

"Huh, probably sent by my enemies."

Digs looked disgusted. "Listen, brainless, I do have better things to do than wander the desert searching for you, got it?"

Danny averted his eyes and the two fell silent. For a long moment they stood studying the lava sand beneath their feet.

"Um, I'm sorry," Danny murmured at last. "This isn't about you, Digs. Thanks for..."

"Look, forget it. You think you have all the problems? Try being Mexican on an Indian reservation."

"What? Tell me who has said anything to you," he frowned, "We'll kick their butts."

"No, there's no one. Anyway, we'd be the ones with the kicked butts. Can we change the subject? What do we do now?"

"Okay, here's what I'm going to do—hold up here for a few days. That should get them all worried."

They ducked through the doorway into the quiet of the room, sitting next to each other on the mats.

"Sorry, muchacho, they know about this place. Joseph helped you build it, remember? What if they decide to call the reservation police?"

"Let them. I have a clear view down the trail and a special place to hide if they come snooping around."

"Why are you doing this, Danny?"

"Don't you know? You've seen the way I'm treated around here—like a baby," he grumbled. "How many times do I have to get my hand shut in my locker, or my head pushed at the drinking fountain? How many more promises from my dad, only to watch him drive off in his truck? He doesn't care about me...never did."

"Listen, like I said, I get dissed at school too."

"Yeah, no offense, but you're not O'odham. It shouldn't be happening to me."

"Aw, come on, Danny, that's not fair, anyone can be a target."

"Hey, I've never asked for anything special...and it still comes down on my head. And my father...where is he? Well, not anymore. I'm calling this my vision quest. The world will know Danny Rivas as the coyote-meeter from now on."

"Coyote-meeter?"

"Yeah, it's as clear to me now as ever. Joseph says it's a special person who can name an animal as his friend. And my grandfather is called Makai, the healer. No one knows better than he."

"So, you've decided to tell everyone?"

"Yes, and when I get back I'll have finished my quest sooner than anyone else—even some of the high school boys," he puffed.

"What about school? Everyone's getting ready for the Indian Day celebration on Friday. Are you planning to be there?"

Danny scratched his neck thoughtfully. "Maybe I will. And if I show up wearing the trappings of a coyote it would be a lot better than the cornhusk mask I made last year."

Digs shook his head. "I don't know...there's more to think about. Mr. Jensen takes attendance every morning..."

"Hey, no joking. My mom will have to call school anyway, right? What will she tell them, other than I'm sick?"

"You've got this all figured out."

"Pretty much," he answered, "except I could use your help a little."

"What else can I do?"

"You can tell them you searched but I wasn't here. And you could bring me a few things—a blanket and a box of matches would be good."

"Sure, I guess..."

"Oh, and maybe a little food? You could leave it on the big rock by the trailhead at suppertime."

Digs rose to his feet. "Are you sure about this, Danny?"

"About as sure as I'll ever be. Now, you should get going before they decide to come looking."

They left the kih together, walking slowly out from under the ramada. The glare of the sun in late afternoon forced them to shield their eyes. Danny watched Digs as he moved off on the trail. Just as his head was about to disappear below the rise he turned suddenly and called back.

"We'll always be friends, right?"

He was glad Digs couldn't see his tears. He nodded and waved, before turning his back again on the outside world.

4

Stones scattered and dust billowed as the Chevy pickup wheeled sharply into the driveway. No sooner had the truck lurched to a stop than the driver was out the door, slamming it behind him. He pulled the cowboy hat off his head, whipping it against his leg in frustration.

"He wasn't there?" Cecilia asked from the step. "Was Digs home?"

"One question at a time...No, Danny wasn't there," answered Tony Rivas. "Or at least, Digs didn't seem nervous enough to be hiding him. And yes, I know where he is." He stopped to stare off into the desert.

"Well, are you going to wait all night to tell me? Where is he?"

"Don't get excited, he's fine, according to Digs. I had to grill him pretty good to get an answer."

"I'll get excited," she shot back, "and it would be nice if you did too."

He flipped the hat back in place, yanking on the brim. "Listen, Cil, it's been a tough day and I'm beat. He's run off before. If you think I'm going out there to look..."

She barely heard him speak. "Yeah, running off...just like you've been doing every day of your life."

Tony's lip curled. "W-What are you talkin' about?"

"Aw, I don't believe you. You know exactly what I mean... your job, or your so-called job."

"Hey, I work hard every..."

"And where are you after work? Your work is a mystery, Tony...when it starts and when it stops...where the money is."

"I-I do the best I can."

"Walking in after dark with beer on your breath is the best you can do? Day after day...How many times, Tony?"

"Yeah, so I guess..."

"You guess, all right." Cecilia's eyes flared. "You've never had time for Danny. And what have you been teaching him all the while? Run away...just run away from your problems, your responsibilities. Really good, Tony. Why don't you just belt down another Tecate with the boys?" She began to cry.

"Calm down, will ya?"

"I won't calm down. And I bet he isn't fine either. If he were fine he'd be home here where he belongs. He was hurt, Tony. I'm not making this up, I saw him."

"Huh, not hurt so bad he couldn't tear off like a roadrunner. He's over at Sheep's Head Rock in the shelter, which means he has water, probably a fire, and he's out of the cold."

"So your plan is to leave him out there?"

"For the time being, yes. I want him to stew a little. I would imagine he'll get some help from his pal, too."

"This is amazing," she glared. "Some father...letting your son live in the desert like a wild animal. We need a change around here, Tony...and we need it now."

"Okay, Cil, that's enough. You know very well that he loves the outdoors. It's an easy one for him. Besides, he expects someone to come after him. Let's see what happens when we don't."

"What about school tomorrow?"

"So he misses a couple of days. All they do over there is color and paste anyway."

"Yeah, mister smart Indian," she huffed. "If you ever helped Danny with his homework you'd know how hard the math is these days."

He stepped past her, pausing to hang his hat on the wall peg and untie the laces of his work boots. Plunking wearily on a stool, he pried them off with his toe. He was careful to avoid her stare as he placed them neatly against the wall.

"That's it...walk away again."

His lip was tight and he didn't answer. The air hung thick with tension from their battle of wills and the heat of a long Arizona afternoon.

"I'm starving...what's in the icebox?"

"I wouldn't have a clue," she growled. "You'll have to figure that one for yourself."

Dusk had descended as he approached the trailhead on the outskirts of the village. House lights blinked from beyond fingers of whisker cactus, casting dark shadows across the path. He moved in a silent crouch, hoping the dogs in the yards wouldn't sense his presence and launch into choruses of barks and yelps. One sound that seemed to thunder in the night air was the growling in his stomach.

Okay, Digs, the moment of truth...Did you leave any food?

When he spotted the blanket roll lying on the boulder he forgot all about the pain in his knee and the throbbing in his forehead that returned every time he exerted himself. His feet churned in the loose gravel as he scrambled to reach the prize.

He was greeted at the rock by the noisy yap of Pepito, the Chihuahua, bouncing up and down on his leash in the Delgado's backyard. Grabbing the bundle, he ducked behind the stone where he sat grimacing with pain. Thanks to his use of the yucca compress, the gash in his leg had begun to heal. But it looked like the running had opened the wound again. A trickle of blood oozed from the deep cut. He rocked back and forth holding his knee, trying to listen for sounds from the house. The tiny dog continued to yip and whine nervously.

Minutes passed without a response from inside. This wasn't like the Delgados to let the dog bark, especially at night. Danny decided to risk a quick peek at the yard. From around the edge of the boulder he could see figures moving about in the bright light of the kitchen. It looked like the Delgados had company and the evening meal was in progress.

Mr. and Mrs. Delgado had been the Rivas's neighbors for many years, but Danny didn't feel he knew them very well. They were much older than Cecilia and Tony, and pretty much stuck with their own generation. Before he retired, Mr. Delgado had driven a truck for the Pima County Department of Transportation. He was a stout muscular man with long gray hair worn in a single braid. In spite of his overall grumpy attitude (Danny swore he had kept his baseball once after it ended up in his yard), he had shown kindness by helping Tony with his pickup when it wouldn't start.

Attached to the rear of the house was a small workshop where Mr. Delgado tinkered with an old Ford Fairlane. It must have been ancient since Danny had never heard of a car with that name before. Once or twice a year Delgado even drove it, coughing and chugging, around the reservation just to prove he could perform miracles. He also kept three goats and a brood of chickens within a wire corral near the back fence.

Good, he thought, *they're busy and won't bother me while I check what Digs' left behind.*

Slowly, he unrolled the bundle to inspect the contents.

Inside was a small plastic flashlight, a box of wooden matches, and two Superman comic books tightly bound with a rubber band.

The magazines brought a glimmer to his eye, but it was the small square package underneath that attracted his attention the most. Neatly wrapped in wax paper was a ham and cheese sandwich, along with a box of chocolate Goobers. He raised the treat to his nose, inhaling the sweet smell.

"Mmm, Digs, I owe you."

He wolfed the sandwich in big bites, and then carefully rationed the Goobers for nearly an hour. It was the only food he had eaten all day. The little meal took the edge off his hunger, but he still felt pangs in his stomach. Just then, he remembered there might be fresh eggs unclaimed in the nesting straw of the Delgado's hen house. But in his present condition, could he get in and out of the pen without being spotted? The thought of their hardboiled goodness out of his cooking pot was more than he could resist. He rolled onto his stomach to see past the rock.

There by the back door stood Mr. Delgado unhitching Pepito from the leash. He gently picked up the animal and started down the steps toward the rear workshop. As he walked he gazed casually around the yard, satisfied that everything looked in place. Swinging wide the heavy plywood door, he was swallowed up by the darkness inside. Momentarily, a bright light shone from within, and then his figure returned to the doorway. He lowered the dog just outside.

"Pepito, my little one, not too far and I'll have no more silly barking. Yes, you hear...no silly, silly barking."

The tiny dog pranced happily into the yard. First, darting toward the wire corral, and then making a complete about-face for the house. He raised his leg and peed on the concrete step.

With his gear safely stashed, Danny made his move for the fence along the rear of the property. He limped forward in the darkness, his eyes riveted on the dog. Slowly working his way around a clump of cholla cactus, he dropped to the ground, squirming on his stomach to a spot by the wire.

Now he was directly behind the corral where he could hear the hens gently clucking in the shed. Staring at him curiously from within the enclosure, the Delgado's goats kept watch over the brood.

Rising with a stiff knee, he pushed down on the wire to swing his leg over and straddle the fence. Pivoting painfully, he managed to pull his good leg in with just the slightest shaking of the pen. He stood as still as death, not moving a muscle for fear of alerting the dog. For the longest time he waited, before slowly shifting his gaze toward the yard. Pepito sat at the workshop doorway, his attention focused on Mr. Delgado's activity inside.

Creeping forward, he plunked down behind the coop to catch his breath. The hens grew nervous, clucking and squawking more loudly. Raising his eyes ever so slightly above the roof of the box, he saw Pepito's ears perk in his direction. He ducked down, waiting patiently for the chickens to settle.

When all was quiet he reached inside, feeling for the round shapes in the straw. His hand brushed the tops of a cluster of eggs and he lifted one and then another, softly placing them in the fold of his shirt. When he had collected a few he paused to take another look at the house.

There not more than ten feet away Pepito waited. He watched Danny carefully, his shiny nose pushed through the wire.

Suddenly, the dog's shivering whine exploded in a symphony of yelps and yaps.

Yip, yip, yip, yap, grrrrrr...grrrrr...yap, yap, grrrr...

"Shhhh...Shut up, you little flea bag," he breathed.

"Pepito?!"

From out of the workshop came Mr. Delgado, a donut-shaped air filter in one hand and a wrench gripped tightly in the other. He strode cautiously toward the corral, gazing into the desert beyond the fence.

"Who's there?" he voiced into the dark. "Pepito, shush, shush."

Danny held his breath, shrinking back behind the hen house. His heart pounded furiously and a choke formed in the back of his throat. Sweat dripped from the end of his nose, plopping on the ground like huge raindrops.

Delgado picked up the dog, calmly stroking its head and ears. He stood quietly at the fence listening to the sounds of the night.

"A bobcat or a fox maybe," he whispered to the dog, "but nothing to get excited about." He smiled when he spotted his prize billy goat nibbling on the fence. "Well, Jack, you look worried." He turned away slowly. "Come on, little one, it's past your bedtime."

Danny didn't move until he was sure they were gone. Finally gathering his courage, he peered over the chicken coop at the light still glowing in the workshop. Clinking and rapping noises meant that Mr. Delgado was back at work.

He stole quickly to the rear of the pen, juggling the eggs as he sat astride the fence. A minute later he was back behind the boulder, breathing a sigh of relief and counting his spoils.

"Four eggs made it," he whispered. "Sorry, Mr. Delgado, I'll find a way to pay you back."

Collecting the blanket and other items, he slowly retreated up the path and away from the light of the houses. Beyond the trailhead the slender beam of his flashlight could be seen weaving its way across the desert floor.

5

He eased the pot closer to the coals. As the water inside began to boil, he carefully dropped in the eggs from the previous night's raid. He would eat two for breakfast and save the others in an antelope skin for later in the day. Sitting back from the flame, he poked at the embers with a stick while his thoughts returned to the little ranch house just a few miles away.

"Boy, I bet he was mad when he got home last night. So, what's the difference...never seen him smile anyway. And I bet they had a fight, too. They're always fighting when it comes to me," he grumbled. "Doesn't matter what I say or do, nothing's good enough. I guess I should just accept it."

He peered into the pot to check the progress of his meal.

"But it won't be that way forever—not a chance. Not once word gets out about my quest...and Coyote. People's attitudes will change," he declared. "He won't have a choice; he'll have to smile then."

Once the eggs had cooked he used the stick again to push the coals away. He stared hungrily at the pinkish shells as they cooled in the water.

"Must be it was too late—too dark for them to come looking for me last night. But if they had, I would have been ready to vanish in the desert." He looked out the door of the kih at the morning sun shining brightly. "I'd better make sure to watch the trail, just in case."

Gently plucking the warm eggs from the pot, he lowered them into the olla filled with cold water. Shortly, he could break away the shells and satisfy his appetite.

"I bet Digs was wrong, they don't know where I am. And he would never tell them either...which means a big search to find me. That'll teach him."

Danny sunk his teeth into the yellow center of the egg. He couldn't remember tasting anything so delicious. With his mouth brimming, he focused on a spot where the trail passed between two giant saguaros.

His brow scrunched. "But if Mom calls Grandfather, he will immediately think of this place. Hmm, that's okay though, we are heart-to-heart. I mean, we built this together, didn't we?"

He rose stiffly and stepped out for a better look at the approach to the kih. The wind was beginning to gust out of Mexico. It tossed his thick black hair and kicked up the dust at his feet. He leaned sullenly against the ramada post.

"Grandfather knows every trail in the desert, but his legs are bad. I hope he doesn't try to..."

Whuuump, whuuump, whuuump, whuuump...

He was startled by the sound of propellers rising rapidly over a nearby hill. Ducking inside the door, he watched the approach of a helicopter flying low to the ground. Silver-toned windows reflected the glare of the sun allowing the occupants to closely study the terrain.

He had seen these blue and white-marked machines many times before, crisscrossing the desert in search of illegals. They had even talked about the planes and helicopters at school one day. Mr. Jensen had said they were A-Star 350s, each patrolling with armed officers on board. He told the class that the job of the Border Patrol was difficult and dangerous. Most of the thousands of illegals that crossed the U.S. border each day were not an immediate threat, but it was a serious hassle rounding them up and taking them back to Mexico. According to him, the worst problem was dealing with so-called 'mules'; armed men smuggling drugs, and 'coyotes'; thieves who offered to guide illegals only to steal their money and abandon them in the desert. These were criminals who would stop at nothing to take from others or deliver their deadly packages. But when Danny heard Jensen call such terrible people 'coyotes,' he was very upset. As old Joseph had told the story many times, Coyote had come upon the earth with Buzzard and Elder Brother to shape all the people, the land, and the sky. To join forces with Coyote was a great honor, and Danny knew this in his heart.

He also knew he wasn't dangerous, but would the agents know if they saw him? He hid in the kih as the aircraft's pounding propellers closed above him. Sand blew like a whirlwind about the tiny house while the ocotillo walls shuddered with the force of the downward push of air.

"The smoke from the fire!" he shouted. "I have no choice now…"

He limped from the hut with his arms waving wildly. He had to make them see that it was only he; Danny Rivas, not some drug smuggler. Shielding his eyes from the blowing dust, he watched the copter dip to one side as the pilot surveyed the little lodge in the desert. Continuing to signal, Danny was relieved when the agent finally returned a soft salute. Then, just as fast as he had arrived, the man turned the craft and sped away across the valley.

"Thanks for visiting," Danny called out. "Better you than my father, I guess. Not much chance you'll worry about one little Indian out in the middle of nowhere." He stared at his dust-covered features. "Okay, so I was about to go get fresh water."

Back by the shallow cave he stripped off his clothing, tossing them on a rock. Approaching the hidden pool, he eased gently into the frigid spring water. His breathing calmed as his body adjusted to the icy bath. He scrubbed himself briskly from head to toe, being careful around the area of his wound and applying fresh yucca. When he had finished, he left the coolness of the cave to sprawl on a boulder and let the sun dry him.

Just about noon, he thought, peeking up into the searing rays. *Digs, that means you're about to leave science class at San Xavier School and head for the cafeteria. Let's see, it's Thursday…Oooh, calzones.*

He dreamed of the deep-fried turnovers filled with pepperoni and melted cheese. They were his absolute favorite. Often, the tasty pizza would vanish from his tray before he'd gotten to the end of the line to settle with the cashier. Then, he'd sit in the middle of small talk with Digs while staring hungrily at his friend's food. It never worked though. Digs was much too smart (and hungry) for that.

Sometimes two other students in their class would take pity on their souls and sit near them. Nick Peters and Theresa Cerona weren't so bad. In fact, Danny thought Theresa's brown eyes were beautiful.

The more he thought about it, the more he realized that the loneliness of his flight from the village was beginning to have a negative effect. At first, being by himself had seemed like the right thing to do—the only thing to do. But now he found himself talking and complaining out loud. It was embarrassing to think that this behavior was actually stealing his pride away. Cursing his solitary vigil, he turned onto his stomach to let the sun warm his back.

"Huh, and tomorrow is Indian Day. I guess I won't worry about showing up," he announced. "I might be coyote-meeter, but I don't have time to make a proper costume."

His body jerked at the sudden sound from behind. Whirling about, he stared wide-eyed at Digs Ramirez standing beside him. A toothy grin covered his pal's face.

"Nice outfit," he chuckled. "Why don't you wear that tomorrow?"

"Hey, don't sneak up on me like that. What are you doing here? School's not out yet."

"No duh. I skipped out...right after science. I told the nurse I didn't feel good. Ms. Valencia wrote me a pass in the office."

"Yes, but she'll call your house, dummy."

"This is true, Tonto...and leave a message which I'll erase long before my parents get home."

"So, fine, but you've got no business skipping and scaring the life out of me."

"Ha, *me* skipping? So what's your excuse?" he smirked.

Danny eyed him coldly. "Excuse...? What would you know about it? Listen, you want to hear a good excuse, ask my father. That's all he's got."

"Well, that's not my p-problem. All I know is you're not my boss, so stop acting like some friggin' big shot."

"All right, I won't," he barked, kicking at the ground angrily. "Oww!"

"Huh, you should put on shoes before you try that—and your pants too, if you don't mind."

Danny's defiance began to melt. Slowly, a smile crept across his face. It was his first smile in a long time. Leave it to Digs, he thought, to relieve his hurt, even for a moment. He punched his pal's arm and then covered up playfully when the smack was returned.

They cuffed and slapped at each other, thankful that the spat was over. Digs grabbed Danny's jeans from the rock and tossed them in a nearby prickly pear.

"There, that should make those a lot more comfortable," he laughed from a safe distance up the path. "I'll be at the hut."

"I'll remember this," hollered Danny, unable to control his snickering.

When he returned to the kih he found Digs sitting on the mat drinking from the clay pot. He sat across from him motioning for him to share his drink.

"I forgot to thank you for leaving me the stuff," said Danny.

"Don't mention it, amigo. But now the question is; how long are you planning to hold out?"

He shrugged his shoulders, reaching for the pot. "Well, uh ...Dunno, hadn't really thought about it."

"Um, I hate to break it to you, but I don't think anyone's going to come looking. I've already said your parents know you're out here."

"Yeah, I figured," he frowned. "I wasn't sure at first, but..."

"Listen, it had to be your father's idea to leave you stranded. I'm sorry, man—he really got in my face. I would never have told, if that amounts to anything." He watched him closely. "So, what now?"

Danny studied the mound of white ashes in the fire pit.

"This is supposed to be my vision quest, you know."

"And what have you learned?"

He frowned at Digs. "Answers don't just fall from the sky. I've only been out here one day."

"Sorry, I guess I don't know much about this sort of thing.

Anyway, you're the Indian...Isn't it something you learned from your elders?"

He nodded, "Yes, and Grandfather told me this time wouldn't be easy."

"Then, I should keep bringing you food, right?"

"No," he said, "I didn't mean it that way. Listen, here's what I'm going to do. I'll wait another day for Coyote to return."

"Well, what if he doesn't?"

"Uh, then it won't matter because he's already saved my life once."

"Huh? Now, that makes perfect sense to me," muttered Digs, shaking his head.

"My father works on Saturday mornings...I'll go home then. In the meantime, I have two eggs left to eat and then I'll hunt a rabbit. It's the right thing to do."

"Eggs? Where'd you get those?"

"I s-sort of ended up at Mr. Delgado's henhouse last night."

"You stole from your neighbor? How does that fit into your vision quest?"

Danny's eyes dropped. "I-It doesn't. I made a promise to repay him, though."

"Okay, whatever you say, man. Hey, I've got to get back... mi madre will be home soon." He rose and headed for the doorway. "I'm still not feeling well, remember?"

"I remember. Oh, and since tomorrow is Indian Day at school, why don't you start spreading the word that I'm returning from my quest."

"Sure, okay...I won't be in the pageant, but if I tell Nick, he'll get it around in a hurry. Hasta luego."

He followed Digs under the ramada and watched his friend's shadow lengthen against the afternoon sun as he disappeared below the ridge.

6

Cecilia gripped the telephone, wiping tears from her eyes with the back of her hand. "Dad, I don't know what to do," she sniffed. "I'm frantic and I can't think of anything else right now. Danny has been out there for almost two days. He could be dead for all I know. And Tony won't budge."

"What is it this time?" Joseph asked calmly.

"Well, it's more of the same, I'm afraid. Danny's just so angry lately...I-I can't understand it." She started to cry again. "I can't talk to him. He blows up and then he runs. It's l-like he won't let me love him anymore."

"Where's Tony?"

"He's still at work, but he wouldn't go look for Danny this morning. He's still drinking and we had another fight."

"Okay, well...let me finish feeding the animals here and I'll drive over. Do you have any appointments this afternoon?"

"Yes, one in half an hour, but I can handle it," she breathed. "Are you sure you don't mind? How have you been feeling? It's a long drive here from Pan Tak."

"I feel okay—M-My legs are good. In fact, I could use a little exercise and so could the White Shadow." He coughed hoarsely into the receiver. "I'll tell Delores not to plan on me this evening...I can have dinner with you?"

"Of course. If there's one thing we have it's food. Why don't you bring Mom with you?"

"Huh, not much chance. Tonight is cards with the girls. I know that Maisy will stay with her if I'm not home until morning."

"Dad...? Thanks, I don't know what I'd do without you."

"Don't worry too much about Danny, Sis. I'd be surprised if he wasn't at the kih. And he did learn from me, remember?"

"Be careful driving," she warned. "You know how fast they go on eighty-six."

"White Shadow is long and wide. She will carry me safe and unafraid," he answered.

"My dear, that old car is a clunker."

"You'll see. I'll be there before you know it. Watch for me about three."

She hung up the phone and walked quickly out the front door. Her eyes scanned the sagebrush and mesquite trees dotting the desert floor. The wind had died across the top of the greenery and the birds seemed strangely quiet.

"Danny...wherever you are, please be strong and know that our Joseph will find you."

Santa Ana winds blowing hot and dusty through the canyons had all but erased the trail toward Sheep's Head Rock, yet Joseph picked his way along the trace without hesitating. Gripping the gnarled end of his walking stick, he maneuvered around massive boulders and between giant saguaros, stopping only once to drink from the goatskin slung on his shoulder. How magnificent were the thorny heights of his old friends! The twisting arms of the two hundred year-old cacti rose like fingers of Mother Earth high into the sky.

"We are still here, my brothers and sisters. But you are so great, and I am like an ant crawling," he sighed. "And you will not wait for me, will you? You will live on when I must return to the East. "WuD hab masma o hemhowa, as it must be."

Ahead lay the higher ground where he and Danny had built the kih. In spite of the steep grade, he pushed on bravely, his back to the afternoon sun. He was determined to find his grandson and ease the suffering of his daughter.

Danny eyed the ocotillo stem all the way to its tip. He frowned at the natural bend still in the shaft. In spite of fierce whittling with his jackknife, he had been unable to straighten it.

"Ayee, you will never fly right," he complained. "You wobble and shake like you are a nervous ocotillo. What must I do...throw you away from the rabbit so you will curve and strike it?"

He sat cross-legged by the fire pit, dipping the green point of the spear in the flame to harden it. Beside him rested three unfinished lances; all rejected for the same reason. When he had practiced firing them at a prickly pear pad he had missed every time. It was a very good thing his grandfather was not around to see these new weapons, if it was possible to call them that.

"Maybe I should start with an easier project," he muttered, "like a toothpick."

He sniggered at the thought as he whittled along the trouble spot. At least the shaft was smooth and the point was sharp.

"I could use it to hunt the baby rabbit."

"The baby rabbit is hardly a meal," replied a familiar voice from the doorway.

"Grandfather!" he cried. Tossing the spear aside, he climbed to his feet and hobbled stiff-legged to hug the old man.

"What are you doing here?"

Joseph held him tight, patting his back with an arthritic hand. They stood in the shadows unable to break the bond that had joined them for so long.

"Oh, I thought I'd admire our handiwork one more time," he said, gazing around the dim interior. "And I can see that you and your friend did a fine job finishing the roof."

Danny beamed. "Yes, Digs and I...Well, it was mostly me..."

"I see, I see..."

"And look at the grass bundles, Grandfather. We tied them just the way you told us to, leaving the smoke hole."

"You have laid them neatly as well. I noticed the smoke draws out nicely. So, you have not made the ceiling too high. It is a kih to be proud of, my son. And it is built in the way of the first desert people."

"Ha," Danny gloated, "even better than the one at the Cultural Center Museum."

Joseph eyed him shrewdly. "Good enough to be honored on Indian Day."

"Today is In..." Danny's face began to redden.

"And I hear the parade at the mission this morning was a long one. They say everyone marched in costume from the school all around the square. Did you wear your cornhusk mask?"

Danny stared down. "You know I wasn't there."

"I know only what you tell me," answered Joseph.

"Okay, well I wasn't, Grandfather. I-I decided to...go on my vision quest instead." He studied him carefully. "You mean Mom didn't send you?"

"I am not sent by anyone," smiled Joseph. "I am a healer... I go where I am needed."

"Um, I h-have this bad cut on my knee..."

"It looks as though you cleaned it in good fashion. Did you apply a compress?"

"Yes, I used the milk of the yucca."

"That is good," he nodded, "you have done a makai's work. Now your body must do the rest."

Danny seemed satisfied. "So, that's pretty much it. I've started my quest and...Boy, am I glad you're here, Grandfather."

"I am also happy about our time together. You know, Danny, the body and the mind are one."

He squinted at Joseph. "What do you mean?"

"In order for your knee to heal properly—for your body to be well—your mind must will it."

"So, you mean my body does what my mind tells it to?"

Joseph chuckled. "Yes, that is true...at least until you get to be my age. What I really meant was your mind is at the center of your universe. If it is sick then the rest of you will be sick, too."

"I-I think I understand. But my mind isn't sick...Is it?"

"No..." he answered. "But you wanted to be at Indian Day today, didn't you?"

"Uh, y-yeah, I guess."

"Does it make you sad that you weren't?"

"Yes, sort of—Yes, I'm sad..." His eyes looked vague, distant. Momentarily, he turned back to the spear tip, rubbing it nervously.

Danny's expression worried Joseph. "Then we will get to work—just you and me," he said, hugging him close. "I see you have taken good care of the olla. And those ocotillo spears are well made..."

"I love you, Grandfather."

"I love you, too," Joseph answered softly.

7

"They're all straight now," he marveled. "How did you do it?"

Joseph nodded quietly. "It is about knowing where there is too much and too little. Practice—the experience of time—also matters. If you fall, you must be prepared to get back up." He handed him the last of the ocotillo spears.

"Were your first spears worse than mine, Grandfather?"

"That was so long ago, but I think so..."

He laid his head on Joseph's shoulder. "How did you get so smart? Did you hang out with your grandfather?"

"I did as a young boy...until he left for si' aleg weco, the place beyond the eastern horizon."

"What kind of place is that," asked Danny.

"It is a land beyond the stars where all O'odham people go when their life on Mother Earth is finished."

"Wow, he must have been really awesome. Was he...a great chief?"

"Your great, great grandfather was named Manuel. He was a farmer who came here from Mexico many years ago when the United States government started the Sells Reservation. He took his living from the land, which is not an easy thing to do. Yes, he was a great man and a leader among our people."

"What about your father?"

"I learned the most from him," Joseph answered. "I think that was because my blood was closest to his. Whenever I wanted to know something I asked him and he always tried to answer me."

"Yeah, I wish...Dad could be like that."

Joseph's gaze fell heavily upon him. "You wish Tony could be like what?"

"Smart like your father, is what I'm saying."

"So, you don't think he's smart?"

"Well, no, I don't mean that exactly..."

"Danny, maybe what you mean is you haven't asked lately. Do you think that's true?"

"Huh, I can't ask him anything when he's not home."

"Ah, then the problem is not about getting answers, it's about spending time together, right?"

"Yes...Yes, that's right. He's not there...He's never there, because if he was it would mean he cared. That's how I see it, anyway."

"Sometimes things can be seen clearly, sometimes they are not as they appear. If I promise to talk to Tony about his work will you promise to start asking him again?"

"S-Sure, I'd like that..."

"It is done."

"But, I'm still afraid, Grandfather."

"Afraid of what, my son?"

"His, uh..."

"Be brave, young one, say it."

"His eyes. I-I'm afraid of his eyes...when he comes home. I think he's drunk, Grandfather."

Joseph hugged him in the quiet. A gentle breeze touched their faces through the doorway. At last the old man spoke.

"That will not happen again...I promise you. Never...do you hear?"

"Yes, I hear." Danny buried his face in Joseph's shirt. A tiny sob escaped his lips.

After a time, Joseph released him, gazing down fondly. "Good, it's settled then. Come on, let's go to the spring for fresh water."

Collecting the olla and the clay pots, they left the kih and threaded their way through the rocks to the secret pool. In spite of his advanced age, Joseph kept a steady pace, never losing sight of Danny. Ducking beneath the overhanging ledge, they crept across the sand to the water's edge.

"Ah, the tracks of Coyote," noted Joseph. "It looks like we are not the only visitors."

Danny smiled broadly. "Ha, fooled you, Grandfather. I made the marks with my finger. It must be they look real or else you would have known."

"Well, they sure do. But if I look close I can see that your paw is too big, and the imprint is too deep in the soil. If this was truly

Coyote he would be the giant brother of I'itoi."

Danny's smile slowly disappeared from his face. "The thing is...he is real. And he saved my life."

"What do you mean, son?"

"I-In the wash below Little Wild Horse Canyon."

"Hmmm, yes, a place I know well."

"I forgot about the danger. I wasn't paying attention and I got caught in a flood. I thought I would die for sure."

Joseph frowned. "When did this happen?"

"Before lunch, on Wednesday." He looked up sadly. "I thought I would never see you again, Grandfather."

"Wednesday...?"

A sudden shiver ran through Joseph's body. He gazed in silence across the glassy surface of the spring.

"Are you okay?" Danny asked.

"I-I am fine now. But now is not the issue. Wednesday— middle of the day—I h-had this attack...a spell, or something. Your grandmother was afraid. She thought I had a stroke, maybe."

"But you didn't, right?"

"No, just this loud buzzing in my ears. It was the sound of bees. After a while it went away." Joseph wiped a light sweat from his forehead.

"My ears were buzzing too. Right before I got caught in the tree. And then I heard the growl of a coyote."

Joseph rose quietly, walking out from under the ledge. He stood watching a bank of cottony clouds drift across the sky.

"Tell me what happened with—Coyote."

"Well, i-it was big, really big...almost like a wolf, and it had dark fur."

Joseph sat next to him. "He came to you along the bank of the wash?"

"No, he was in the tree. We were both caught in a dead tree."

"I don't understand."

"A snare, Grandfather. The line from a snare was wrapped around him and tangled in the tree. I grabbed the rope and he pulled me free. He saved my life—and I s-saved his..."

"Chekaidkam ban," he chanted.

"What was that?"

"One who can hear Coyote."

Danny shook his head. "But we can all hear coyotes. Some nights they yap up a storm out here."

"Not in that way. You have met Coyote and he is brother of the Creator." Joseph hugged him reverently. "You are the coyote-meeter now."

"I-I am? Yeah, I am!" he cried. "I knew it, Grandfather, I just knew it!"

Cecilia waited patiently on the step as Tony's truck and low bed trailer rumbled into the driveway. She could see the tired look in his eyes, but thankfully, nothing else.

Must be he heard me when I said we needed a change, she thought.

His weak smile told her he wanted to make up after their fight. She watched him grab his hat off the dash and slowly step from the truck.

"Hi, babe," he breathed, wiping grime from his face with a neckerchief. "I'm pooped. Do we have any cold water?"

"Yes," she answered, smiling quietly. "I-I'll get it in a second. Here, gimme them shoulders..."

He plunked wearily beside her, letting her strong fingers work the muscles in his back. Gently rolling his head, he tried to loosen the tight cords in his neck.

"Any news about Danny?"

"Not yet, Dad's with him," she said.

"Yup, I see the car. You mean to say Joe went out there in his condition?"

"He's a lot better lately. Hey, never underestimate his herb and root garden. Not to mention that he always makes a come back when he's with Danny. You know that."

He sighed heavily. "Yeah, that he does. I'm assuming he'll spend the night with us. I don't want him out driving on the road tonight."

"Yes, he's got the old couch. But Tony, don't you think you should head out toward Sheep's Head Rock to meet them? I know you're tired, but…"

"Hmm, well, with two of them out there I guess I'd better. And my fathering hasn't been much to brag about either. Damn, we just can't seem to stay caught up."

She hugged his arm. "We'll find a way. You just start thinking of Danny first, okay? Sophie and I are making your favorite meal tonight. Dad loves them too."

His brow perked. "Stuffed chiles?"

"Did you need to ask?"

He leaned and nudged her ear with his nose. "Sorry about this morning. I just couldn't pass on that job."

"Uh-huh, so take an extra jug of water with you. And your flashlight might come in handy, too."

"Looks to be an hour or so of light left…I think I'll head out." He stood stiffly, flexing his lower back. "Try not to worry if it gets past dark. Joe could walk that trail with his eyes shut."

He disappeared into the house and returned a short time later with a camouflage print backpack. A pair of hikers had replaced his work boots.

"Be careful, Tony. We've had warm days lately, so watch for rattlers."

"Huh, mess with old coontail? Not me."

He turned with a wave and headed into the desert, disappearing in a maze of sage and cactus.

8

Joseph nodded, "It is a great honor to have such a powerful ally in your life. And he who has met Coyote shall bear the name and be remembered by all of the people i'ajeD, from now on."

"Way cool," Danny bubbled. "Then I must be a pretty important person, right?"

"Well, you are one person among all the O'odham. There are others who have met Coyote—and who will meet him in the future, perhaps." His eyes narrowed. "But I have only known one before you. It is more about responsibility to honor Coyote by living your life in a certain way."

"But I didn't mean to meet him."

"You cannot plan such a meeting," Joseph answered. "Neither can you shirk the responsibility once it happens."

"What should I do then?"

"You should be proud to take up the task. Let me tell you the story as I have heard it." He watched the light slowly fade outside the cave. "And we should say goodbye to our kih for now. Cecilia and Tony are very worried about you. It is time to go home, don't you think?"

They gathered their belongings and stored them in the back of the room. With a promise to return for a summer sleep over, they set out on the trail in the shadow of Sheep's Head Rock. As dusk descended they passed among the saguaros into the valley below.

"Very long ago a baby was born to Mother Moon on a mountain called Sun Striking Mountain," Joseph began. "But she was so busy giving light that she could not feed the child, so she hid the baby in the tall grasses of the desert. The child was left to survive on the food of the earth. And do you know who this child was?"

"I think he was Coyote," said Danny.

"You are right. One day he approached the dwelling of Earthmaker and Buzzard. He was immediately known by them and called by name, Coyote. Together they met a powerful and mysterious being named I'itoi who was greatly feared. When he demanded they call him Elder Brother they quickly agreed. With Buzzard flying overhead, they traveled the earth together accomplishing many good deeds. All the time, I'itoi and Earthmaker argued over who was best."

"I bet they caused storms and stuff when they fought."

"It is true that Earthmaker's angry hollering is the thunder, and I'itoi's boasting is the wind. As it is with all the people of the earth, those who are most powerful have the greatest obligation to those who are least powerful."

They continued along the zigzag of the trail showing pale in the moonlight. Joseph used his walking stick like a snake does its tongue; testing the path ahead by flicking and probing at unknown shapes.

"There are always two thorns for the night traveler to avoid," he cautioned. "Those of the prickly pear are everywhere and are like the needles in your grandmother's sewing basket, while the thistles of the cholla are little cowards that hide in your skin."

"Tell me more about Coyote, Grandfather."

He placed an arm on Danny's shoulder, halting him on the trail. Together, they lifted their eyes to gaze into the night sky.

"Once, without thinking, I'itoi caused a huge flood that sent the people fleeing into the mountains. The waters rose so high that all were drowned and the birds flew to the top of the sky and hung on by their beaks. The flood reached the tail of the woodpecker and you can still see the marks on it to this day. Then, I'itoi, Earthmaker, and Coyote made a pact that whoever came out of the water first would be called Elder Brother. Earthmaker and Coyote were the first to come out and I'itoi was last. But I'itoi insisted again and was allowed to take the title."

Danny looked puzzled. "Why did they keep giving in to I'itoi's demands?"

"Well, even though Earthmaker was really stronger, he didn't realize it, so he falsely feared I'itoi. And since I'itoi was not of their kind, they didn't truly know him and decided to be generous."

"Hmm, so I should be generous to strangers?"

"You can be kind and giving with one eye while cautious with the other."

"That's what Mom tells me, sort of."

"After a little while they decided to make more people to replace those who had died in the flood. So they took clay from the moist ground and started to make dolls. When they had formed a few, they looked at them and Coyote's were made the worst. Earthmaker's were not very good either, and so they accepted I'itoi's because his were made in his own image. It was they who shaped the world and brought people to live on the earth. Coyote followed them as they scattered people all around, poking his nose into everything."

Danny grinned as the scene unfolded in his mind. He grasped Joseph's hand, guiding him around a sprawling manzanita bush blocking the trail.

"Your stories are awesome," he said. "How is it you can remember so much?"

"I only tell about what I know to be the true way. And what is right in your heart is never lost from your mind."

"I think my parents believe I've lost everything from my mind. All they do is criticize. But I can do things." He looked up at Joseph. "I'm good at a lot of stuff, right?"

"Truer words have never been spoken, my son."

"Would it be okay if I came to live with you and Gram for a while?"

"Your home and my home will always be the same, but I think Coyote is asking you to face your problems squarely. Running from them is like running from yourself. Do you agree?"

"Y-yeah, I guess."

Joseph patted him on the neck. "I believe you have been chosen for something important. We must live out the days to discover what it is."

Danny's attention was suddenly drawn to a spot of light moving in the desert ahead. He watched the tiny beam swing from side to side, sometimes shining more brightly.

"Grandfather, look...a light. There is someone else on this trail tonight. Who could it be?"

"It is hard to know, but I think we will soon find out."

Danny's eyes grew wide with fear. "We're not far from the border. Could it be an illegal? Or maybe even a drug smuggler?"

"I hope not to meet such men," Joseph murmured, "for I have heard they are evil."

"Wow, should we get off the trail and hide?"

"I think that would be wise. We shall get out of his way and let him go about his business." He held tightly to Danny's arm. "Over there...that boulder. We can stand behind it and listen for his footsteps to pass."

They moved quickly into the shadowy brush, winding among dark clumps of sage and creosote. Arriving at the rock, they huddled quietly against its rough surface.

"In a minute he will be within earshot, so we must remain very still," whispered Joseph.

"I'm scared, what if he finds us?"

"Don't worry, my son, the desert will protect us tonight."

In the stillness Danny listened to his heart pound. He pressed against the stone, closing his eyes tightly. Just then he heard the light tramp of feet approaching. From Sheep's Head Rock, the howl of a coyote suddenly pierced the night air.

9

A chorus of lonely yelps followed, echoing across the valley floor and off the walls of distant cliffs. The howling brought a halt to the pad of footsteps on the trail.

Danny held his breath, listening. He could feel the tightness of Joseph's arm around him. It seemed the silence lingered for an eternity. And then he heard scuffing on the path and with it the sound of a man's voice.

"Huh, you guys are a little out of tune tonight, aren't you?"

"Dad...?"

"Whoa," Tony voiced. "Who's there?" His flashlight shot up, sending a beam out into the darkness. "D-Danny? Joe?"

Joseph's hold on the boy loosened. "Yes, it is us," he answered. "Here, behind the rock. Lower your light, we are coming out."

Carefully threading their way through the undergrowth, they were soon back on the path. They stood quietly by while Tony panned his light across their features.

"I don't believe you two," he said, "walking around out here in the dark."

"It looks as though you are doing the same," Joseph noted.

"At least I came prepared." He wiggled the flashlight in his hand.

"Well, Danny has a small one if we need it, but we are near the trailhead, and the desert is my home. I know it as I do the rooms of my house."

Tony eyed his son nervously. "A-Are you ready to come home? Cecilia has been very worried about you."

"What about you, Dad? Were you worried, too?"

"Y-Yes, of course I was." He stared down at the ground. "Listen, so it was my idea to let you sit on this for a while. Do you understand why I wasn't going to come running out here after you?"

"Um, Grandfather sort of explained it," Danny replied, "about my new responsibility, that is."

"Responsibility? What do you mean?"

He smiled proudly. "I'm the coyote-meeter now."

"The coyote...?"

"Yes, we saved each other's life. And so I must be a leader and follow his example."

Tony eyes followed Joseph's gentle nod. "Okay, t-that's fine," he decided. "I assume this means to do better in school and not run away again?"

"Yeah, but I *have* been doing well in Mr. Jensen's class. And I love going to the kih. Grandfather can build the best in the world."

"All right, but spouting off at your mother and doing the jack rabbit routine isn't going to cut it, understand?"

"I understand," he glowered.

"Now, what's this about Mr. Jensen's class?"

"We started this cool stuff on astronomy a few weeks ago. Mr. Jensen says we're lucky to live here in the desert because the sky is so clear for star watching. We had a big test the other day, but we haven't gotten it back yet."

"We can talk of this at the dinner table," Joseph inserted. "I don't know about you, but I could use some of my daughter's cooking."

"Not a bad suggestion," said Tony. "Come on, Cil's stuffed peppers are getting cold."

They started back, guided by the beam of the flashlight.

Where the trail widened, Joseph caught up with Tony.

"We should talk together of certain things," he whispered.

The seriousness in his tone was all Tony needed to hear.

Explanations weren't necessary, especially with the problem so out in the open and obvious. Danny's actions had made it so. He nodded that he understood. They didn't speak as they trudged on; with Danny nearby this wasn't the time.

Crossing the ridge, they saw the scattering of village lights in the distance. Their pace quickened as the chime of the bell in the mission tower faithfully called them home.

Part Two

Joseph

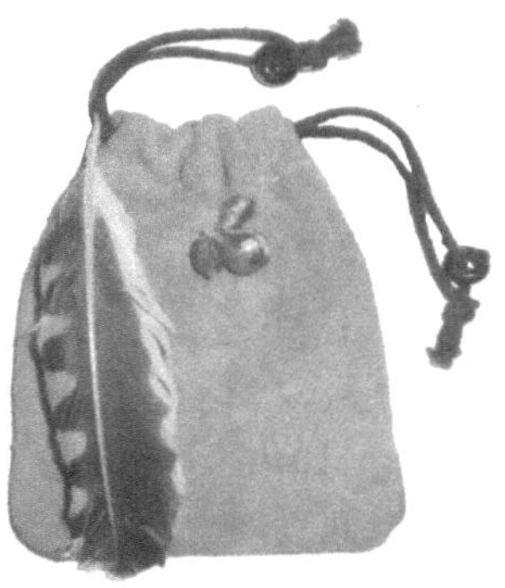

10

A cool breeze rustled the curtains in the Rivas's bedroom windows. With it came the morning sounds of birds singing in a nearby palo verde. Along the fence where the yard met the desert, cottontails scurried into the shade of sprawling buckwheat and agave. All about, signs of a new day abounded, when suddenly the chirping died away, replaced by an uneasy quiet.

"Danny," whispered Joseph, prodding his sleeping form, "wake up, I have something wonderful to show you."

"Wha...? Grandfather, please, I'm so tired."

"Quickly, my son, he is like the phantom. To see him is a gift offered to few." The old man nudged him excitedly. "Please, come."

Danny sat up slowly, stretching and blinking. His sleepy eyes gazed about the room, finally focusing on Joseph's face.

"What is it?" he croaked. "What time is it?"

"It is early, but there is no time to explain."

"Okay, okay..."

With a bit more nudging, he was soon creeping with Joseph through the house and out the back door. As they crossed the yard they stayed hidden behind a cluster of fruit trees. Joseph stopped several times to peek through the leafy branches at something in the desert.

"We must stay out of sight of the boulder at the trailhead," he warned. "Come, we are almost there."

"Why are we sneaking around the backyard? Are you okay, Grandfather?"

"You will know in a second why we must be so cautious."

Dropping to their knees, they crawled forward beneath the last of the trees. There they waited in silence, their eyes riveted on the magnificent form lying atop the rock.

"Holy..." Danny breathed. "He's huge."

The mountain lion's tail flopped lazily from side to side as he watched them from his perch. His nose tested the air, gathering in human scent.

"If we do not move,' Joseph murmured, "his instinct will tell him we mean him no harm."

"Us, h-harm him?"

Joseph eyed the cat warily. "Unless he is very hungry, he will search for easier prey. Besides, there is a more important reason why he is here now."

"Why—why is he here?"

"He is here for water, my son."

"Water? I don't understand."

"The drought has been many months," Joseph sighed, "many years..."

"What can we do, Grandfather?"

"There is nothing we can do. His spirit rests with Hewel, the wind, and with Elder Brother."

Danny's lips quivered. "But what if he dies?"

"He will never die, that I can promise you."

Without warning the cat sprang up, shifting his weight toward the desert. He stood motionless for a time watching the distant hills. Once more he looked back at them, baring his teeth in a phony display. And then lifting from the boulder, he shot across a ten-foot span, landing silently on the lava stone track. Veering off the path, he slipped effortlessly under a thorny oak and vanished into the undergrowth.

"Wow, he jumped so high."

"It is a great day, Danny. I have lived a long time and never seen Mawid in the wild before."

They sat with their faces to the wind, listening to the birds resume their peaceful chorus. Soon they were awakened by the sound of kitchen clatter and the smell of fry bread and bacon wafting across the yard from an open window.

"That's making me hungry," said Danny. "What about you?"

"Between Delores and your mother...it's amazing I don't weigh three-hundred pounds. Come on, let's go."

"I talked to Digs yesterday," Cecilia announced, staring awkwardly at her plate. "I was just concerned that you were all right."

Danny peeked at her shyly from across the table as he stuffed honey-dipped fry bread into his mouth. He hoped things wouldn't get emotional again this morning, but he realized she was still upset over his two days in the desert. Thanks to Joseph, the first few minutes of table talk had been friendly and comfortable.

"Uh, yeah? What did he say?"

"He mentioned the soccer game at school this afternoon against St. Augustine Middle. He wondered if you would be there."

Danny's eyes lit up. "Yeah, sure, I was planning on maybe going."

"Well, not so fast," piped Tony. "Your mother and I talked last night about a consequence for your running away."

He looked quickly into his lap. "I p-promise I won't do it again."

"Okay and we've heard that one before. So, here's the deal. You're grounded for two weeks."

"Aw, Dad, that's a long..."

"Beginning tonight after supper," he added. "And believe me, that's your mother talking, not me. I wanted it to start immediately."

Danny glanced at Joseph, but the man's gaze remained fixed on his plate. He munched quietly on his food.

"So that means I can go to the game?"

"What did I just say, son?" Tony asked. Before Danny could answer, his father's finger shot up. "But don't push it."

"Okay...okay, I won't push it," Danny mouthed weakly.

"Now, I didn't know what to tell Digs," Cecilia said. "You'll have to call him and ask him to meet you at the field."

"Cool."

"The game is at two, right? But remember, you must be home to begin your sentence as soon as it's over. And don't bring Digs along, either."

"I wasn't going to," he muttered.

"Hey, chin up," said Tony. "It could be a lot worse, you know." Wiping his mouth, he rose from the table and started for the denim jacket hanging on the wall peg. "Sorry, Babe, I know it's Saturday, but that Parker job. I should be home by mid-afternoon."

There he goes again, thought Danny. *Gee, Dad, when do I get some time?* He poked dumbly at a bacon crumb on his plate.

"Joe, are you okay driving back down eighty-six?"

"Yes, Tony, I'll be fine."

Tony shook his head. "Boy, how in the world do you keep that old car of yours running?"

"The White Shadow does not fail me because I have faith in it," Joseph answered. "We are old friends—the engine and me."

"Does it talk back?" Tony asked, grinning.

Cecilia rose and gave him a gentle push. "All right, go. That job won't get finished if you stand around."

Joseph suddenly rose and followed Tony out of the kitchen. He stopped him by the screen door.

"I will not return to Pan Tak until you and I have talked,' he braved.

"Yes, I know," said Tony, scratching his neck.

"So, when will it be?"

Tony hesitated. "Uh, I think now would be good. Come on..."

The two moved quietly down the steps and into the gravel drive. Joseph spoke as they walked.

"I will not hold back, Tony, this you must know." He grabbed the man's arm and held on firmly. Tears began to well in his eyes. "You bring dishonor to our family...and yourself."

"You've been talking to Cil..."

"Yes, but talk was not necessary. I could see the pain in the eyes of my daughter and my grandchildren."

"I-I..."

"You have nothing to say now, only to listen." Joseph's hands trembled and his voice cracked with emotion. "Cecilia, Sophie, and Danny are mine too...as close to my soul as the spirits of our people. Danny means more to me than life itself."

He moved closer to Tony, looking hard into his eyes.

"You will never again disrespect my family with alcohol or excuses. Am I clear?"

Tony looked away sourly. The pressure from Joseph's grip was unrelenting. After a time, he tried focusing on the old man's face.

"I know I-I've been wrong," he stammered. "And I have made a promise to myself to try to change."

"You will do more than try, my son," Joseph shot back. "You will succeed, or else there will be no protection for your soul when you journey from Mother Earth...or for your body while you still walk on it."

"I-I..."

"We will speak no more of it," Joseph whispered softly. The talking is finished...and the doing has begun."

Tony felt Joseph's grip relax. He nodded quietly and turned toward the pickup, parked in the shade of a mesquite.

Danny watched curiously as Joseph returned to the table. His grandfather looked composed and his expression was calm. Just before he had left and after Sophie had excused herself to her room, Danny had noticed the perfect chance to break the news to Cecilia. Now he nudged Joseph's arm eagerly.

"You won't believe what we saw this morning."

"Don't tell me," said Cecilia, "there was a fox in Mr. Delgado's henhouse."

Danny's fork clattered to his plate. "Uh, hardly," he coughed, glancing at her nervously. "It was a mountain lion, Mom, a real, honest-to-goodness mountain lion. He was on the boulder out back."

"Really? Gracious, that *was* a sight," she replied. "How do you do it, Dad? You always seem to be in the right spot."

"The cat woke me early this morning. I heard him wail in the distance. Perhaps there is also a female about."

"Maybe its better I didn't see him," she said. "That would have been more excitement than I need in one day."

"But there is more, daughter."

"What do you mean?"

He eyed Danny approvingly. "Your son should tell his own story."

"I-It happened a few days ago. You know...when I came home with Digs."

Cecilia grunted. "You mean when you came in all beat up and scraped. You looked like you'd been in a fight with that cougar."

"Well, I did get caught in a wash."

"Yes, and you lost your sneaker, remember?"

"Yeah, Mom, listen," he breathed, "I almost died."

"You what?" She studied him fretfully.

"But I didn't. That's the thing—I didn't. I was saved by a coyote."

"A coyote? Oh, now that's crazy. How could a coyote save you?"

Joseph cleared his throat. "Cecilia, please. Give him a chance to explain."

"You see, I was trapped in the branches of a tree with the water pouring all around me. And so was Coyote...trapped, that is. Someone had tried to kill him with a snare, Mom. It was all wrapped around and he couldn't move. That is, until I untangled him. I was careful not to let go of the rope. And then he pulled me loose."

She shuffled her feet uncomfortably. "That's quite a story. I suppose you think it means something? I mean, otherwise, why would you worry me so?"

"Because it's really important, that's why."

"Well, I don't...Dad, you're obviously involved in this. What's going on?"

"Cecilia, I would rather let Danny tell you, but it is basic and you should already know. Your son is now the coyote-meeter. And among all the O'odham people this is an honored thing, is it not?"

"Well, yes, but this sounds like it was accidental..."

"Daughter, nothing is by accident. Coyote is our reflection in the still waters of a lake that helps us walk the good, red road. He is our most powerful teacher, and he has come to Danny to be his ally in life. There is purpose here and we must respect this situation."

She studied him warily as she collected the plates from the table. "Sometimes I wonder, Dad, how well the old jives with the new."

"It has always been good in my life. I think there is no other way."

"So, you understand, right Mom?"

"Okay, I guess there's no denying you had a spiritual experience. And if so, then isn't Coyote asking you to look at yourself in some way? I would say this is more about your responsibility."

"You are correct," declared Joseph. "He must reflect on past actions."

"Good, and how do you think you've been doing lately?" she asked.

Danny rubbed his forehead. "Not very well, I guess."

"Not well is right. I suggest you let this bounce around your brain for a while this afternoon. Let me know what sort of answer you come up with."

"Okay..." he whispered.

She smiled at him over her shoulder. "Oh, and your meeting with Coyote does make me happy. Really, Danny...It's true I was mad, but it was an 'I love you' kind of mad. I'm very proud of you."

He hid a grin beneath his hand.

"Now Dad," she continued, "you should call Mom to let her know that you're planning to start back this morning." Grabbing a broom by the icebox, she headed into the next room.

Joseph rose stiffly from his chair. He wrapped an arm around Danny, hugging him gently.

"S-ap, wehs wo/ho wuD, all will be well, my son," he murmured.

11

Danny spotted Digs Ramirez's head well above the others in the group as they huddled in the school parking lot. With the soccer game an hour away, they had gathered as usual to catch up on the latest. He figured there would be serious questions to answer about what he'd done, so he'd arrived early to work on breaking the ice. He approached the crowd cautiously.

"Well, look who's here," chirped Nick Peters. "It's our buddy the dropout."

"Hey," Danny called bashfully.

"I thought you'd died," said Nick. "So, what'd you have, massive diarrhea? Or was it lovesickness?" He wiggled his eyes at Theresa Cerona, standing next to Digs.

Danny's face went red. "Uh, well, neither, I guess. I've just been out in the desert for a while. You know, getting good with nature and thinking about stuff."

"Really? What sort of stuff?"

Danny gave Digs a frown. "Um, certain people were supposed to let you in on my...experience."

"Oh yeah?" Nick looked at Digs curiously. "An experience... cool. So, tell us more."

Danny swallowed hard as his eyes darted among the faces. He was unprepared for this part, but decided not to blame Digs. His friend probably just hadn't found the time—or the nerve.

"I-I had this meeting with a coyote..."

Nick pounced. "Uh, wait a minute. You...had a meeting? With a coyote?"

"Yeah, that's right."

"And who did the talking...you or the coyote?"

Laughter broke from the group as Danny stared about helplessly. Everyone seemed to be enjoying the moment—except for Theresa.

Danny's expression hardened. "Okay, have your fun, Nick. I didn't expect you to understand."

As the snickering died, Nick looked a bit sheepish. "Wow, sorry, I didn't realize you were that totally serious."

"The meeting...it was predestined," Danny declared. "Let's put it this way, we communicated well enough to save each other."

"No kidding? Um, that's just...really great," Nick offered in conciliatory fashion.

But Danny had already moved in a new direction. "Hi, Teri, what's up?" he asked shyly.

"Missed you, Danny," she answered. "You said the desert... where in the desert?"

He studied her face. "Uh, well, I've been staying in a kih near Sheep's Head Rock. I probably would have stayed longer but Joseph and my father showed up."

"Um, really, a kih? You mean like a traditional house?"

"Yes, It's my getaway place. You know, where I can think about stuff. The desert's beautiful and you can see for miles from the rock. I'll take you there sometime."

"I'd like that," she answered. "Is that where your experience was?"

Behind them came the sudden blare of a diesel bus engine announcing the arrival of the team from St. Augustine. The poster-spattered Blue Bird rumbled to a stop by the main entrance to the school.

"Uh, no, it happened in a wash up in Little Wild Horse Canyon," he replied, trying to sound humble.

"You mean you really saved a coyote?" Theresa asked.

"Yup, but more important than that, Coyote saved me."

"I dunno' Danny," inserted Nick. "The way I figure it, animals don't consciously save humans. I think you sort of tricked him with your brain power. Huh, didn't know you had any."

"Listen, Nick, it wasn't exactly like that. Anyway, my grandfather says this is important in my life. And I just know he's right. Very few people get to meet Coyote."

"Hasn't happened to me, I'll give you that."

"Well, not to me either," said Digs.

"Or me," added Theresa. "I think it's, well...exciting, don't you?"

The side door to the gym flew open and several San Xavier players ran out on the field. The team manager trotted behind lugging a net full of soccer balls. The last to exit was Paul Jensen, Danny's science teacher and boy's soccer coach. He walked toward the parked bus to greet the visiting team.

"Uh-oh," Nick murmured. "Here comes someone who'd have trouble spelling coyote."

Ambling confidently in their direction, Jake Boyle and Eddie Vincent had decided to join the group's discussion, invited or not. When they spotted Danny their heads came together to whisper and snicker joyfully. For them, this was an entertainment opportunity not to be missed.

"Lookie here," spouted Jake, "it's the lost one. Our very own flunky is back. Where you been, ditwad?" He muscled in beside them.

"None of your business," growled Danny. "Can't you tell when you're not welcome?"

"Oh, not welcome...so you own the parking lot, do you?"

"We should have asked for permission first," Eddie chimed.

"Yeah, guess so. Hey, what does it take to get on Jensen's kiss butt list?"

"Why don't you lay off, Jake?" Digs sounded.

"And who's going to make me, Diego?"

"W-We all will," he stammered.

"Haaa, little juhkam boy, little Mexican...Don't make me laugh."

Danny clenched his fists tightly. "That's all right, Digs, I don't need help with this."

"Danny, please don't listen to them," Theresa pleaded.

"Mmmmm, Theresa," whispered Jake. "When are you going to stop hanging with these losers and spend more time with me?"

"Yeah, if ever," she huffed.

The full force of the punch struck Jake's head just below his ear. It lifted him from the ground, sending his body sprawling in the dirt. He sat blinking his eyes, unable to focus on anything around him.

In that same instant, Eddie jumped on Danny's back and they tumbled, thrashing in the dust. Nick and Digs stood over them shouting encouragement.

"Hey, over there!" yelled Jensen by the bus. "That's enough. Both of you cut it out." He quickly covered the distance to the scene of battle. Grabbing them by the arms, he pulled them apart. "Danny and Eddie, what's the story here? And I want the truth."

"I'm sorry, Mr. Jensen," panted Danny. "We were…"

"Uh, they were Indian wrestling, sir," blurted Digs.

"Indian wrestling, my foot. And Jake Boyle, why are you sitting down? You don't look so good."

"I-I…I-I…feel fine…just fainted, I guess." He tried to stand, slipping backward onto his duff.

"Okay, this all looks pretty much like a fight to me. And you know the school rule about fighting."

"Really, Mr. Jensen, it's my fault," lied Digs. "I suggested they try the leg flip and, well, they got kind of carried away."

"Diego Ramirez, that's about the most unlikely tale I've ever heard." He glanced carefully at the others. "Theresa, what did you see happen here?"

Her eyes flitted about. "Yes, I think that's right…Indian wrestling."

A long quiet followed while Jensen took stock of things. But each time he tried to spot dishonest eyes, they were conveniently hidden from view.

"You people are lucky that I'm busy with the game today. Otherwise, I might have handled this differently." He studied Danny closely. "You've been absent from class this week, and on Thursday you missed the astronomy quiz results. That means I'll need to see you in homework club on Monday, no excuses."

"Sure," Danny hemmed, "I mean, yes, I was planning on it."

Jensen addressed the others calmly. "And the same goes all around. I want each of you there as well, got it? I don't care if you're in my class or not."

"Yes, sir," they sounded.

"Now, I'm assuming you came to watch the game. You will follow me over to the field and sit along the sideline. I want to be able to see you the entire time."

Danny walked quietly behind Jensen, sending angry glances at Jake and Eddie. He had to consider himself lucky that his friends had come to his rescue, only it hadn't settled much as far as these two were concerned. He tried avoiding problems with them, but they sure knew which buttons to push. And he was frustrated that he couldn't seem to control his emotions lately, especially around people he liked; Digs, Mr. Jensen—Theresa. What was he supposed to do? He took a deep breath and wiped his face with the bottom of his shirt.

Approaching the sideline of the soccer field, Jensen motioned for them to spread out on the grass. Danny sat quickly beside Digs and Theresa, keeping a safe distance from the others. These were the two people, besides Joseph, who made him feel good, really good. But then, that had been true for as long as he could remember. One thing was for sure; just because his grandfather was impressed and his friends seemed to be, didn't mean the rest of the world would agree. Yeah, he'd experienced something life-changing, and the word of Joseph Estes; respected tribal leader, should amount to something, but it didn't look like it was going to have the effect he thought. His head dropped as he thought of Joseph leaving to drive back home.

"That was a close one, Danny," whispered Theresa. "You can't let guys like Jake get to you."

"Yeah, I know," he sniffed.

"Hey, you look so sad. What's up?"

"Oh, I dunno', I was just thinking about my grandfather ...and I'm grounded...starting tonight."

"Ooh, how long?"

"Two weeks. Hmm, that is unless my parents find out I've been fighting."

"Maybe you should give this coyote thing a rest. Bringing it up will just get you into more trouble."

"I-I can't, even if I wanted to. And I don't, really. Joseph says I've been chosen for something. It's like a gift. I can't help it if others aren't impressed."

"Well, I think it's pretty cool. Hey, if it happens, it happens." She nudged his shoulder. "In the meantime, just get back to your normal self, will ya'?"

A half-hearted smile was all he could muster. He appreciated her being a friend, he really did, but when it came to closeness, no one could compare with Joseph.

"Okay, are you ready for this, genius?" asked Nick, sliding beside them. "Word is you got the highest score on Jensen's science test last week. He showed us the curve and there was one grade above ninety-five. When we asked around we drew a blank. That means it must be yours."

"No way."

"Dude, I'm serious, all the papers are back except yours."

A smile crept across Danny's face as he watched two San Xavier players advance the ball past mid-field.

12

Afternoon sunlight streamed through the classroom window onto Danny's paper. The glare broke his concentration, forcing him to shift his chair. He peered in frustration at the grammar samples printed neatly on the page. Why did Sister Margarite have to make these so difficult? Finding a verb wasn't bad, but when it came to identifying the subjects in each...well, that was nearly impossible.

"Get this over with," he prayed, "so you can do your math."

Across the lab sat Jake Boyle, exercising his brain by counting the ceiling tiles; first, from the front of the room to the back, and then, hallway door to window. He kept a noisy tally as he worked.

"Jake, please," begged Jensen, "don't you have something else?"

"I did it all in study hall, Mr. J."

"Well, thank God for study halls," he noted softly. "It's almost three-thirty, so I'll let you go a little early. If you see Eddie Vincent let him know I haven't forgotten. Being absent doesn't excuse him from homework club."

"Gotcha' sir," he responded, pointing at Jensen as he strolled out the door.

Danny used the sun excuse to peek at Theresa sitting in the front row. Each time he caught her eye she wrinkled her nose. This was an activity far more interesting than grammar _or_ math. Unfortunately, Jensen's voice interrupted their long distance communicating.

"Mr. Rivas, could you give Diego Ramirez the same message? I swear, you guys give 'I don't like Monday' a whole new meaning. I wonder why? Oh, and come up a minute, please. I have a test score to discuss with you."

His heart leapt as he prepared for the news. He watched the excitement grow in Theresa's eyes as he approached the front desk. Trying not to grab the test from Jensen's hand, he searched the top of the paper for his grade.

"Mr. Jensen, I-I don't understand, there's no sco…"

There it was, underlined in blue half way down the right margin—97. He stared trance-like, barely aware of the adult voice trying to reach him.

Jensen waved in his face. "Hello, Earth to Danny."

"Gee, I'm sorry."

"You know, I had to search hard to find a mistake anywhere. You did a really excellent job. In fact, I'm seeing strong evidence that your math skills are starting to pay off in science, too. What do you think?"

"Wow, I guess so," Danny answered shyly. "Learning about astronomy is way cool, especially the stuff you showed us on star groups and measuring distance."

"Well, I'm glad, very glad. So, here's what I'd like to propose…" He spotted Theresa listening in. "And do you mind if a certain young lady hears our conversation?"

"N-No, not at all, sir," he answered, watching her smile widen.

"I didn't think so. You know, you two spend an awful lot of time staring at each other."

"Mr. Jensen?" Theresa uttered.

"Sorry," he chuckled, "I just like to help people out any way that I can."

"Y-You were saying…" interrupted Danny.

"Yes, okay, what I'd like to do is challenge you a bit more with an independent project. Are you interested?"

"Sure, I am. What sort of project, Mr. Jensen?"

"I have a university friend who works over at the Kitt Peak Observatory. He has an advanced degree in astrophysics."

"Uh, astro…what?"

"Astrophysics, but don't let the word scare you. He knows about the unit we're studying and asked if I would do him a favor. He's looking for two temporary lab assistants to help him around the station. Not much for details right now, but I'm thinking it would involve some routine cleaning, chasing around, you know."

Danny's eyes grew wide. "Really? Kitt Peak? Cool!"

"And here's the coolest part of all. You'd get to be around some of the world's most powerful telescopes directed at planets and star systems millions of miles from Earth."

"Oh, wow," he beamed. "Did you hear that, Teri?"

She nodded excitedly, "yeah, that's amazing, Danny, just great..."

"I wish I could offer you the other opening, Theresa," Jensen added, "but I have to go with my top math student, Alex Winterbottom. I'm sorry."

"Me too," Danny murmured.

"That's okay, Mr. Jensen," she said, "I'm kind of busy as it is."

"Well, thanks for understanding, and Danny, you should also understand there are some academics involved. At the end of the month I'd be expecting a detailed poster project and a class presentation. The subject would be up to you."

"Great, when can I start?"

"I'll have to check and let you know. So, sounds like I don't need to do any further convincing."

"Yup, I mean, nope," he sputtered happily.

"Then that's it for today," he said. "Oh, and please keep this between us until I formally announce it to the class, okay? You two are dismissed and good job, Danny, one more time."

She watched his face as they walked the dimly lit hallway.

His smile had become a look of anxiety, and it was clear all was not well in his mind.

"Alex Winterbottom is pretty nerdy, but you don't really know him do you?" she asked.

"Aw, he's no problem...other than he talks to himself all the time."

"So, what's up?"

"I just remembered I've been grounded for two weeks."

"Ooh, that's right, but your parents will understand, won't they?"

"Teri, you don't know my father."

"But for something this important?"

"I'm telling you, he said no to the soccer game on Saturday, and that's not all..."

"What do you mean?"

"Well, I-I knew it wasn't right to miss class last week, but he didn't seem to care. A-And I've heard him before—dump on school, that is."

"I thought you said he came after you at the kih?"

"Yeah, right," he huffed. "Joseph came to Sheep's Head Rock, not him. He was on his way Friday night, but I think they were more worried about Grandfather than me."

"Come on, don't be so defensive."

"Sorry," he said, shaking his head, "it sort of comes with experience."

"Listen, I like your parents...your mom especially. She seems great to me, always smiling and friendly."

Danny's lip tightened. "Yeah, I wish that was true, like you said, always. But how often have you been around my father... once or twice, maybe?"

"Yeah, I guess."

"Then you don't know him. He hardly ever has time for us. When he comes home it's usually with beer on his breath. I think he drinks a lot. He'll load up and then go hunting with a couple of friends. They don't come in the house...just wait in the truck. Mom tries to hide it, but I've seen her crying."

"Danny, I'm sorry."

"It's not your worry. Good thing I have a place in the desert where I can go."

Just then, they spotted a human form silhouetted in the light of the outside doors. Something about the person's shape seemed familiar to Danny. When they had closed to within a few feet the figure stepped out of the glare.

"Grandfather," Danny grinned, "what are you doing here?" He ran to the old man, hugging him tightly.

13

"Well, it has been a few years since my last visit to San Xavier School. Do you remember your skit in third grade? Delores and I certainly do." He held Danny close, smiling at Theresa. "And it is nice to see you again, my dear."

"It's really great, Mr. Estes," she answered. "I-It's an honor, really."

"Hmm, more of an honor for an old man to be with two such beautiful children."

"I have some awesome news, Grandfather."

"As I have for you, my son, but first we have our friend to think of. It is Theresa?" he asked.

"Yes, you remembered, sir."

"I will be taking Danny home with me. Can I offer to drop you somewhere along the way?"

"That's okay, I live right over by the marketplace. It's just a short walk."

Danny eyed him excitedly. "I'm going home with you...to Pan Tak? Cool. But, why?"

"In a moment you will know," he said quietly.

She looked at Danny. "So, I'll see you at school tomorrow?"

"Yeah, wouldn't miss it."

They left Theresa in the parking lot, climbing into Joseph's old LTD for the ride down state route eighty-six. The power steering belt whistled as the car swung in an arc and lurched onto the highway.

"Whoa, we're kind of swaying, Grandfather."

"The White Shadow has decided to dance in her old age. If she gets it in her mind to do so, I cannot argue. We are lucky she agrees to take us anywhere."

"I see what you mean," Danny answered, gazing at the ancient dashboard, cracked and missing most of its knobs and buttons.

"Now to the mystery at hand," Joseph announced. "If I could remember your friend's name you should remember what is important about tomorrow's date."

Danny's brow wrinkled in thought. "Tomorrow is the twelfth..."

"It happens to me every year on the twelfth."

"That's right," he glowed, "it's your birthday! I almost forgot. Happy birthday, Grandfather."

"Thank you, and do you know how many saguaro harvests have come and gone in my lifetime?"

"Um, fifty?"

"Ho," he chuckled, "I would agree that fifty years is a long time, but for me it is more like eighty."

"Eighty? Holy..."

"And to help me celebrate all those harvests, you will stay with us until Sunday. We'll have a picnic at Peña Blanca Lake with all the family. How does that sound?"

"Great, but what about Mom and Dad? I'm supposed to be grounded you know."

"I have talked to them," he assured. "I will be in charge of your grounding. Besides, who would deny me my birthday wish?"

"Well, I sure wouldn't."

They grinned at each other across the broad seat of the car. As the sun dropped lower in the sky, the faded Ford rumbled onward. Over the tops of ridges and down into the bottoms of washes, it carried them deeper onto the reservation. They slowed along a thicket of gramma grass to watch a desert tortoise amble off the edge of the pavement.

"Life in the fast lane," smiled Joseph.

"Man, is he pokey," Danny added. "You'd think he'd move a little quicker to cross such a dangerous highway."

Joseph followed his progress with amusement. "Buzzard has taught him to save his energy until he finds nourishment again.

In the desert it is difficult to find food and water. For him, life's walk is a long one."

"Then that's pretty smart, right?"

"Yes, and he will live many contented years as a result. Things cannot be rushed," Joseph noted. "It is important to think about each step. And speaking of steps...how is it with you? Has your life been moving too fast lately?"

"Y-Yeah, well you know. Ever since I met Coyote, that is."

"Then it's possible you have missed the sign he left for you."

Danny frowned. "I don't see..."

"Coyote is asking you to look at your situation. He sees things are out of balance in your life, and he wants to know what you plan to do about it."

"I-I don't know what to do."

"Yes, I understand, my son. But you should also know I have spoken with Tony, and much of this is not about you or the blame you have accepted."

"Well, I..."

"You are not to blame," Joseph whispered. "Do you understand me?"

"What s-should I do then?"

"Let us go slowly and plan how we will journey on the good red road, while your father does the same. Elder Brother sees something very special in you. Do not forget that you are O'odham and these are your people."

They fell silent for a time, observing the beauty of the passing landscape. A yellow sign ahead warned of 'open range,' and while Joseph watched the road for stray cattle, Danny let the hot breeze of the desert whip at his face. He thought about Tony, Cecilia, and Sophie—about how things had changed lately in the family. Was it wrong that he had run away? As Joseph had said, only the passing of the days ahead would tell. What mattered to him now was being with his grandfather. He never worried when they were together. He felt safe, like a fledgling quail following its mother as it explored the desert for the first time.

"Oh yeah, I almost forgot," Danny voiced suddenly. "Mr. Jensen is getting me a job at Kitt Peak Observatory. Isn't that cool?"

Joseph's eyes brightened. "It is, indeed. And how did this come about?"

"Well, it all started when I got my science test back this afternoon. I got a ninety-seven, Grandfather. Amazing, huh?"

"Not so amazing...you are gifted, as I have said."

"And since I did better than anyone else in the class, I got chosen for this special project."

"Oh? What is special?"

"I'll be doing some important research with the big telescopes up there," he beamed, "and then reporting back to the rest."

"Most impressive," smiled Joseph. "Will you share your findings with me, too?"

"I'd be happy to, but remember I'll be doing pretty complicated stuff."

"Ah, that's fine. I'm sure you'll be able to explain it to me in a way that makes sense."

They did a high-five. "Yes, I guess I could."

The battered sign whizzing past read Pan Tak, but the White Shadow never slowed in its late-day safari down the deserted highway. If Joseph had missed the turn by accident he certainly showed no interest in turning the car around. His gnarled hands gripped the steering wheel and his eyes watched the road ahead intently.

"Weren't we supposed to turn back there?"

A thin smile appeared on Joseph's lips. "Normally, yes, but today is not a normal day."

"I don't get it," frowned Danny. "What's not normal?"

"It would be better to say what is special," he answered. "I have an old friend in Sells I would like you to meet."

"Aw, Grandfather, do we have to? I'm getting hungry. I usually have a snack after school."

"Snacks can come later. We may not get this chance again, my son."

"Really? Well, what's the rush?"

"The rush is that Jonathan is the oldest of the O'odham and his health has been very poor lately. I sent word that we wished to see him and we are lucky he has agreed to meet."

"Who's Jonathan?"

"He is ge'egeD, Jonathan Luhya Gray Horse, Elder of the Tohono O'odham. Many say he has seen one hundred winters."

"Wow," Danny uttered, "he's like tons older than you are."

Joseph smiled widely. "Indeed. He spoke once at Tribal Council of his father meeting the great Theodore Roosevelt."

Danny marveled at the thought. "Theodore Roosevelt? Wasn't he like a Civil War soldier or something?"

"Yes, or something. He was President of the United States more than a century ago. Jonathan still has the presidential medal Roosevelt gave to his father."

"Sweeet, can we see it?"

"It is possible, but we will let Jonathan decide."

"That's cool, so where does he live?"

"Just past town is a narrow road that leads several miles into the desert. We must watch for it carefully." The old man glanced at him warmly. "So, how is your hunger holding out?"

"I guess I can make it, Grandfather...Yeah, I can."

14

Rap...rap...rap...rap...rap...rap.

The engine knocked loudly as the car climbed the hill, bumping and pitching along the rocky track. Danny watched a giant cloud of dust billowing behind.

"I thought you said this was a road," he coughed, wiping tears from his eyes.

"Not all of Arizona is a freeway," Joseph answered. "And Elder Brother would say that is a good thing. Hang on, there is a ledge ahead."

Cruuuuuuuunch.

"I think that was the exhaust pipe, Grandfather."

"Not to worry, we'll pick it up on the way back."

"How does Jonathan get food and stuff way out here?" asked Danny.

"Well, there is little a man of his age needs, and I should know. Ha, success."

Chugging over the summit of the ridge, they spied a low adobe building nestled against the cliff wall. A wisp of smoke snaked skyward from a bent stovepipe. Hanging in loosely tied bundles from a ramada were grasses, herbs, red peppers, and strips of antelope jerky drying in the sun. A brood of chickens raced from beneath the front bumper as the car ground to a halt in the yard.

"Look," Danny grinned, pointing at a wire pen, "he's got a goat just like the Delgado's."

"And what were you saying about his food?" asked Joseph. "We will ring that old bell on the fence before we go in."

At a glance the homestead looked ancient and weather-beaten. Chunks of adobe had worn from the corners exposing the wattle and brick underneath. The corrugated metal roof was rusty and torn at the eaves. A broken windowpane had been plugged with cardboard, while the heavy oak door sagged and creaked on its hinges.

Danny cautiously followed Joseph's lead into the dark interior of the house. The heavy smell of mesquite wood filled the air in the one large room. In spite of the glow of hot coals in the woodstove, the space was cool; separated from the heat of the desert by thick walls. A hand-woven blanket, beautifully designed, hung in a drape across a stone archway. From a squeaky rocker by the stove they heard a raspy voice call out.

"J-Joseph? My eyes are not so good. Please..." A bent figure gestured with a crippled hand.

Danny felt himself being pulled toward the chair. Peeking around Joseph's arm, he gazed numbly at the face of the old chief. The elder's skin was wrinkled and leathery with a hooked nose and bloodshot eyes. Danny noticed a strange cloudiness covering his pupils. His pure white hair hung below his shoulders in ragged fashion.

"Yes, Jonathan Gray Horse, I am here. It is good to see you," said Joseph, "and I have brought my grandson."

"Ohh?" The chief's expression brightened. "Well, have him come here."

Danny's heart pounded and his legs shook as he stepped forward. He forced his mouth and cheeks to smile.

"H-Hello, sir, I'm D-Danny," he gulped, his brain suddenly running in reverse. "It's an honor to meet someone as old as you."

Jonathan's aged lines cracked in a grin and his eyes twinkled through the milkiness. He leaned close, clutching the boy's hands in his lap.

"And how did you know, son of sons?"

"Know what, sir?"

"That I was so old," he chuckled.

Danny's face turned a deep red. "I'm sorry, I didn't mean it like that."

"Do not be sorry. It is an honor for me to meet one as young as you. And you are right...I have stayed long upon Mother Earth. But I feel the night is descending."

The chief's gnarled fingers warmed Danny's hands. "Oh, there's still another couple hours of daylight, I'd say."

Jonathan cackled joyfully. "Too bad our paths did not cross earlier, for you speak a wonderful truth." He nodded at Joseph. "Where have you been keeping him?"

"All to myself, I'm afraid," he said. "And you should also know that he is the coyote-meeter."

Gray Horse's eyes instantly narrowed as he tried to focus on Danny's face. He reached up to pat the boy's neck.

"This brings gladness to my heart. We should remember this happy visit then, yes?" He reached inside his shirt. "I have something here for you, young Daniel."

Jonathan held an antelope skin pouch tightly in his hands. His fingers trembled as he inspected the soft sack, turning it slowly and with great reverence. He loosened the leather tie to reveal the contents, carefully placing each object in his lap.

"These crystals have the winter of Baboquivari in them," he murmured. "See how they sparkle like falling snow? Their light lays bare the soul, and you are wise to abide by these truths."

He picked up a tiny feather, handing it over gently. "Do not fear the owl for he is master of the night and will guide you to the light of dawn. But be sure to thank him for sharing his time as he is busy hunting for the mouse."

"It's so small."

"It is Kuhkwul, the elf's feather, and size is less important than swiftness and a sharp claw," Gray Horse replied. "And speaking of sharp..."

"Oh, cool," piped Danny, staring at the bird talon in the chief's hand. "Is that from an eagle?"

"It is from the sharp-shinned hawk. He will carry your prayers to Elder Brother, my son."

A tiny red stone in his lap had almost gone unnoticed. It dropped suddenly to the floor, rolling next to Danny's foot.

"Here, I've got it," he said. He held it close to his eye, studying the deep color. "This is perfectly shaped, like a marble."

"I have kept it many years. It is from the wall of San Xavier Mission. The Spanish used stone from the Santa Cruz River in the adobe of the church. It is a reminder to us O'odham that we have had to share our land."

Patiently returning the items to the pouch, Jonathan drew it tight and handed it to Danny.

"I don't know what to s-say…"

"Say nothing, but take it and keep it with you always."

"Grandfather, look," he uttered, holding high the sacred bag. "Isn't it awesome?"

"More awesome than you might imagine, as it contains the power of the desert and the spirit of our people," reminded Joseph. "It is yours until the day you choose to part with it."

"Are you kidding? I'll never part with it."

Gray Horse smiled broadly. "Then I am pleased it is to your liking. All will be well with you, Daniel."

From inside the old chief's shirt came the glint of silver. Danny peered shyly at the shiny disc hanging by a beaded cord.

"Is that the medal from the president?"

Jonathan held up the heavy badge for him to inspect. "A picture of Jefferson given by a Roosevelt," he mused, "to my father in nineteen hundred and two."

"That sure looks like solid silver."

"Yes…"

Joseph placed a hand on Jonathan's shoulder. "I think our young one has great enthusiasm and has enjoyed this time."

"No more than I," answered Gray Horse.

"Jonathan, is there anything we can do for you before we leave?"

"Huh, I am in need of little. I have meat and goat's milk. And Alita from the Council brings me fresh tortillas."

"Then I will add some wood to your fire."

With a blaze crackling in the stove they headed quietly for the door. Danny turned to look once more at Jonathan Luhya Gray Horse, oldest and wisest of all the O'odham. The old man's voice resounded from the back of the room.

"Peace on your journey my new friend, Coyote-meeter."

15

The car lurched along the rutted road toward the outskirts of Sells, the largest of the many settlements on the Tohono O'odham Reservation and the seat of tribal government. Danny had visited the town on many occasions to participate in Indian Day celebrations, watch San Xavier sports teams play at the school, and visit the Venito Garcia Library with Cecilia and Sophie where they would take turns using the computers. He also liked rummaging through the young reader books there for adventure stories and mysteries. But after a long day at school and a drive in the desert to meet the old chief he wasn't interested in the library this time around. He was hungry and tired.

"Can we stop at the store? I need a snack."

"Yes, I could use a fresh orange to satisfy me until I get to Delores's cooking. How did you like meeting Jonathan?"

"I liked it fine. He seems very wise and he gave me this..." He studied the medicine bag closely. "Grandfather, will you live as long as he has?"

Joseph smiled from behind the wheel. "I am nearly there, but at my age I take nothing for granted."

"I don't want you to ever die."

"Only the Creator knows when a person's time has come to pass to the East. But those who love life should not talk of this for it is sure to bring sadness."

"Okay, then at least not for quite a while."

"I will do my best, my son."

Danny's eyes followed the gentle curve of an ocotillo fence as it passed his open window. Everywhere in the village, rows of the thorny stalks surrounded small flat-roofed houses. He studied the mostly empty yards wondering what the kids who lived there were doing on a Monday after school. One thing was for sure; they weren't receiving gifts from honored tribal chiefs like Jonathan Gray Horse. Reaching over the seat, he stashed the antelope pouch in the front pocket of his backpack.

"Anyway, thanks for taking me up there. It was cool. I can't wait to tell Digs and Theresa."

"Do you think they'd be impressed?"

"Well, I know Theresa would. And speaking of my friends, how will I get to school this week if I'm staying with you?"

"Do not worry," he answered, patting the dash, "the old white school bus will carry us to the mission each morning."

"Are you sure that's okay, Grandfather?"

"I'm as sure as I can be. The White Shadow is an old horse in need of exercise, and it will give me an excuse for spending more time with Cecilia."

In the gas station store, mostly empty at suppertime, Joseph stood at a cooler by the door sorting through limes and oranges. Next to the checkout, Danny plucked a Snickers bar off the candy rack. A heavyset man with long braided hair peered down at him from behind the counter.

"You've got money for that?"

"S-Sure, I'm with my grandfather," Danny said, motioning across the room.

The clerk did a double take. "Joseph Estes is your grandfather? All the O'odham know of him."

"Really? You mean we're famous?"

"He is famous, it is true. But I have never seen you before."

"Well, I'm Danny Rivas, the coyote-meeter."

"The wha...?"

"The coyote-meeter," repeated Joseph, approaching the counter. "Coyote has saved the life of my grandson."

"Uh, that's...terrific," the man said. "I didn't know coyotes could do that."

Joseph held up his hand reverently. "They can if hewel, the wind, is favorable, and if the situation is under the watchful eye of I'itoi, protector of the O'odham."

The man hesitated. "Y-Yes, well, I guess that's true, especially if you say so. My memory's not so good...you know, from my days of schooling."

"I am only too pleased to help you remember," said Joseph.

"Okay, so, an orange and one chocolate bar, that'll be seventy-five cents, sir."

Danny's eyes never left him as they passed beyond the glass door. There he stood, still clutching Joseph's change in his hand.

Climbing back in the car, Danny looked worried. "He didn't seem to care...kind of in a fog, wasn't he?"

"Yes," agreed Joseph, "I'm afraid some on the reservation are like that now. It is distressing to me...but, do not let it change your thinking, my son. Remember the words of Jonathan Gray Horse."

"I will," he nodded, "I will..."

He sat in silence with the Snickers bar tucked in his pocket all the way back to Pan Tak.

When the lunch bell rang the following day, Danny breathed a sigh of relief. After a morning like he'd had, how could the afternoon get any worse?

To begin with, Joseph's strange chanting over the car engine had somehow gotten it restarted after it stalled along the highway on their way to San Xavier. And so, having arrived twenty minutes late for homeroom and without his notebook, he'd missed the announcements (fortunately, Theresa was there to fill him in). While the rest of the class exited the door for first period, he was left to frantically scribble the homework assignments on the back of his hand. Then, right on schedule (it never took her more than twenty-four hours to correct even the longest assignments), Sister Margarite returned their Monday grammar papers.

Hooray! The number of correct sentences had been neatly circled in red at the top of the page! While Theresa sat next to him admiring her perfect '10,' he stared woefully out the window—a gigantic number '2' pulsing in his head.

All through the second half of language arts he'd sat in a cloud bank thinking about Jonathan Gray Horse and the antelope pouch he'd received as a gift. It was still secreted away in his backpack, safe and sound until he needed it, or in case he decided to share it, although that seemed unlikely.

"How'd you do on Maggie's grammar paper?" asked Digs by the à la carte counter.

"Next subject," he sighed.

"Cheer up, language arts dummy, your math score is at the top of the class."

"Yes, but how good does an 'A' look on your report card with an 'F' next to it?"

"Come on, you won't fail. The final test is in a few weeks. That'll save you."

"I-I sure wish I could believe you, but it'll take more than that, I'm afraid." He peeled the hoagie roll back to reveal three soggy meatballs. "See those? That's how my day is going so far. Boy, do I need science class."

"Huh, you'll get over it," Digs replied. "But here's something I can't get over...you actually want to go to Jensen's class?"

"Are you kidding?" Danny mumbled, taking a hungry bite of the sandwich. "Science is really great...interesting, you know?" He munched away thoughtfully. "Hmm, and speaking of interest, my parents...my dad especially, seemed to show more when I talked to them on the phone last night."

Theresa slid in next to him. "I kinda' heard that. Gee, that's great, Danny. You see? I told you to keep up the spirit. Oh, and don't worry about Sister Margarite, I'll help you study for her test. We'll kick butt." She pushed her mashed potatoes onto his tray. "Here, help me eat these."

"Hey," Digs grinned, "at least Ren and Stimpy over there are leaving you alone."

Danny spotted Jake and Eddie sitting in a group by the door. They were taking turns filling their mouths with milk and letting it drizzle down their chins amid wild laughter.

"On a brighter note," smirked Digs, "I sort of overheard Alex Winterbottom talking about the Kitt Peak assignment. He was telling some kid that Mr. Jensen would announce it today."

"He did, huh?" Danny peeked at Theresa. "Cool, now we're talking."

They ate quietly for a moment watching two boys at the next table flipping a paper football. When one's field goal attempt split the other's finger goalposts, it struck him squarely between the eyes. "It's good!" yelled the kicker.

"And how's the grounding going?" asked Digs.

"Um, well, I'm sorry we haven't talked. It's going okay...my grandfather came and picked me up. I'll be staying with him in Pan Tak until Sunday."

"That sounds a little boring."

"No, he's really great. This morning when our car died on the way to school, he did a chant over the engine and it started right up. I think the car listens to him...it's happened before.

And yesterday on the way to his house he took me to meet Jonathan Gray Horse."

"Who's that?"

"Wow, I know him," said Theresa. "That is, I've heard of him. Isn't he like our greatest chief and really old?"

"How does one hundred sound?" Danny crowed softly.

"No way," scoffed Digs.

"Yes way, he has a medal given to his father by Theodore Roosevelt. Joseph told me presidents used to award them to important chiefs...as a way to gain their confidence."

"So what was he like?"

"He lives alone in a canyon above Sells. He's nearly blind, but still gets around okay. He's very smart, but also very mysterious."

"Whoa, were you scared?"

Theresa responded, shaking her head. "I also heard he's a makai, a holy man. There's no reason to be afraid of them."

"Yes, just like my grandfather. And when Joseph told him I was Coyote-meeter he treated me with respect."

"Really," Digs voiced, "even a great chief?"

"Yes, really. I wouldn't lie about something like this."

"Danny, we're on your side, you know that," said Theresa.

"Yes, but I don't know about some...even my mother didn't believe it at first. Joseph says he spends more time teaching than he does healing these days."

She lowered her voice when a group down the table started listening. "Just keep believing in yourself, that's what's important."

He gave her a quick smile. "All I know is I love my grandfather. He wouldn't steer me wrong."

Danny looked forward to Mr. Jensen's science class. He had a knack for corny jokes and 'failed' lab demonstrations. The best part was deciding if that little explosion or liquid turning barfy green was supposed to happen or not. He was good at hiding the facts, always doing it on purpose to force his students to think. He also had a great way to make sure students were listening; first, he asked a question, and then he added someone's name. No one knew when it was their turn—very tricky. He was a performer and Danny loved his act.

"Okay, guys, as you know," Jensen began, "there are nine planets orbiting the sun. This week we are concentrating on the two closest. And those two would be...Eddie?"

"Uh, w-what was that, Mr. J?"

"All right, it appears those meatball subs you all had for lunch have had a damaging effect on your physical and mental well-being. The problem is far more serious than I thought." His eyes scanned the faces of his students. "I don't get it, I ate two and I feel fine."

A happy grin erupted on Danny's face amidst a chorus of giggles from around the room. He liked it when Jensen included the whole class in the joke. It made him feel relaxed—sort of respected, and he worked better that way.

"So, what we'll do is change topics and get back to Mercury and Venus later."

When Danny saw Jensen glance in his direction, he knew the time had come for a special announcement. His legs fidgeted under the table.

"It's a pleasure to recognize two San Xavier students who are currently maintaining an 'A' average in core math and science. They have been selected to participate in a unique opportunity at Kitt Peak National Observatory beginning this Thursday. For the next two weeks they will work after school with my friend and colleague, Dr. Steve Richards, a professor at Arizona State University in Tempe. They will be working around one of the world's largest telescopes...the four-meter Mayall Reflector."

Jensen waited patiently for the buzz of excitement to quiet. He walked from behind his desk and stood among the tables.

"At the completion of their assignment they will be presenting to the class. I would ask them to stand, please....Alex Winterbottom and Daniel Rivas."

16

The rest of Danny's week in Pan Tak went quickly, especially the first two afternoons at Kitt Peak Observatory. He thought Dr. Richards was way cool. He explained things to make it easier to understand and he told funny jokes that were almost as good as Mr. Jensen's. As far as Danny was concerned, anyone who could get Alex Winterbottom to laugh had to be a true comedian. And as he waited for Joseph to pick him up outside the telescope tower, he had to admit he was beginning to like Alex, sort of.

But the best part so far had been looking at images through a telescope of the night sky over Arizona. Dr. Richards had just shown him pictures of Spica, the brightest star in the constellation Virgo. He thought it was interesting that this 'star' was actually two stars close together. When he learned they were more than two hundred and fifty light years away he was amazed. And when Dr. Richards reminded him that one light year was nearly six trillion miles, he seriously considered doing a somersault!

So if this was such fun, why was he suddenly feeling a little weird? He decided it had to do with Joseph, strangely enough. It was hard to put a finger on it, but when he had reported all the excitement of the first day to his grandfather, his reaction had been a bit peculiar. Instead of a happy grin and a pat on the back, it had looked more like a forced smile—not exactly the old Joseph he knew and loved. Maybe he just didn't appreciate science. Danny wasn't sure, but he hoped today would be different.

Rising from the curb at the familiar sound of a broken muffler, he watched Joseph pull in front. Although it was kind of early to tell, his expression seemed contented and cheerful.

"How did it go at the giant star gazer?"

"It was awesome, and I like Dr. Richards, too. He's a lot like Mr. Jensen." He dropped wearily into the seat.

"Makes for a long day, huh? It's sort of like going to two different schools."

"I guess so, but Mr. Jensen said it was learning by doing, you know?"

"I'm afraid I do not know much about school today," Joseph admitted. "It has been many years for me. And the little woman who was my only teacher left with the spirits long ago. I-I am a man of the past, I'm afraid."

Danny eyed him curiously. "Well, any person can learn, Grandfather. School may be different now, but it's nothing to fear."

The words were no sooner out than he thought of what he'd often said about himself—the dumb punk thing. He immediately began to blush.

"What is wrong, my son? You don't look so good, all of a sudden."

"No, I-It's okay, I'm fine."

"Maybe you heard the howl of a coyote?"

"No, well, maybe. It's just that...wow, I think I'm pretty confused right now."

"Do not be confused, we follow the right road."

"That's just it, which road?" he sighed. "I mean, we were talking about science, and then Coyote..."

"Danny, science feeds your mind, and Coyote feeds your heart. Choosing a road is something for the heart."

"But I love science, too."

"I do not argue," Joseph murmured. "I only remind you that Coyote is near. He has walked into your life and is asking you to look at something you have been avoiding. We have talked of this, haven't we?"

"Yes, but..."

"Then as before, we will let time pass until an answer becomes clear. And remember, Cecilia and Tony are part of this too."

Danny turned away, watching the rocky roadside sail past the window. He had always felt safe and secure with Joseph, and now, he had to add unsure as well.

"You'll help me see myself, won't you?" he asked.

"We take the journey together, beside the reflecting pool and beneath the night sky."

"...so I'll stop giving up, stop running away?"

Joseph's face softened. "I will be blind to what your eyes see, but you will not need me then, my son."

Danny watched him for the longest time as the car rumbled steadily along the desert highway.

Chip...chip...chee...chee...cheeee.

The call of a male towhee sounded about the mesquite thicket as it fluttered and hopped about in search of a mate. A symphony of bird sounds filled the air along the steep wash winding into Peña Blanca Lake.

Sunday had dawned bright and cool; perfect weather for a family outing. As Danny led Joseph and Delores down the path toward the picnic area he realized today would be special for more than one reason. As amazing as it was true, Joseph was celebrating his eightieth birthday and Cecilia and Sophie had decorated the table and surroundings for an old-fashioned waila festival.

Blue and red stars with gold tassels hung from the trees and white crepe paper bows adorned the folding chairs. It all set the stage for a polka-like dance melody drifting from a portable CD player. Danny had heard the familiar accordion, guitar, and drum music before at waila dances in San Xavier. He watched Joseph's eyes brighten with excitement as they approached the happy scene.

"Did you bring your dancing shoes, Grandfather?"

"Yes, and now I understand what is in the mind of a woman," he replied, peeking shyly at Delores. "You made me wear these instead of my sandals. Ho, it is a powerful joining of kindred spirits...you and Cecilia."

She squeezed his arm and kissed him gently on the cheek. They walked in among the family, hugging and laughing as they went.

Amid the chatter and noise, Danny felt a soft tug on his shirtsleeve. There beside him was Tony, reaching out to shake hands.

"Hello, son, good to have you home. Uh, how did your week go?"

Danny's smile couldn't hide the nervousness in his voice.

"It w-was good, Dad. Grandfather and I had fun together. H-Hey, I've been learning a lot at Kitt Peak too."

"Yeah, I was going to ask...what does a young O'odham do around all those fancy telescopes? Come on, let's walk for a minute."

They moved away from the noise, stopping under the shade of an old Palo Verde.

"Well, I've been looking at star systems and planets. I also help Dr. Richards with deliveries and stuff. He's really nice, Dad." His brow wrinkled in thought. "And I do other things to keep busy, like clean the lab..."

"Sounds exciting...listen, son...I-I've been thinking a lot lately about...you and me." He hesitated, scratching his neck uneasily. "I want you to know...that I'm t-trying to change."

Danny couldn't hold Tony's gaze—he stared down at his feet. "T-That's okay, Dad, me too." And then an unexplained rush of emotion brought tears to his eyes. "But...just tell me this...why do you leave? Why do you always leave? Don't you love us, Dad?" He gritted his teeth sadly.

Tony poked about dumbly. "I-I thought you guys always knew..."

"Knew what?" Danny cried. "What are we supposed to know?"

"That I do love you...that I really do..."

They went silent, except for the sounds of birds in the surrounding brush. Danny wiped his eyes hurriedly when the music and the chatter of the picnic began to die. He glanced shyly toward the others and then back up at Tony.

"Um, today is f-for Grandfather. We can't spoil it." He wiped his nose with the back of his hand. "But I never meant to run away..."

"I know you didn't, son," Tony replied softly. "Uh, listen..."

But Danny interrupted—he wouldn't make Joseph wait. "So, w-what were you asking me? Was it something about school?"

90

They turned away from the tree. "Well, the week away with Joe was good. We all agree. It...gave us both some space." He placed a hand on Danny's shoulder. "But there's still a week left on your grounding, you're aware of that?"

"Yes."

Tony nodded quietly. "And what happens when your two weeks at Kitt Peak are up?"

"I have to do a presentation for the class. It's me and another kid...Alex Winterbottom."

"Winterbottom," he repeated. "Don't recognize that name."

Danny shrugged. "He's not reservation. I think he's from Sahuarita or somewhere. So, guess what my average is in science right now?"

"Let's see...Okay, I'd say eighty, like Joseph."

"Eighty, no way. More like ninety-seven."

He raised a brow. "Wow, now that *is* good. You've sure got my old grades beat. And speaking of old...Sister Margarite's still there, right?"

"Yes, she teaches English. Don't you remember, Dad?"

"Yup, well I should I guess. Thing is I spent more time in her room after school than I did in class. I don't think she liked me."

"I-I'm sorry," said Danny. "Maybe school is just different now."

"Yeah, could be. Anyhow, Cil keeps reminding me that I should see your teachers more often."

"That'd be cool," he chirped. "And I can still go to Kitt Peak, right?"

"We've decided it's okay," inserted Cecilia, coming along side. She flung an arm around Danny's shoulder, planting a kiss on his forehead. "Good week with Joseph?"

"Yes, and can we just have fun at the picnic now?"

"You've got it," she grinned. "Come on..."

17

That Sunday at Peña Blanca Lake was one the Rivas family would remember for quite a while, especially Danny, who had never seen his grandfather dance before. And although Joseph forgot the step once while swinging Delores around, he more than made up for it wiggling his hips and his eyebrows. Danny laughed and clapped as he watched, not realizing he was actually smiling with his family for the first time in a long time. He even took a turn himself, concentrating on his feet as Delores talked him through the routine.

By late afternoon, Cecilia's chicken molé with homemade tortillas and Joseph's triple-layer chocolate birthday cake were just pleasant memories in his mind as he helped the family gather decorations and picnic gear for the trip home. He waved happily as the White Shadow carried Joseph and Delores out of the parking lot. From the passing window came Joseph's promise to call him during the week.

A fresh contentedness lingered in the cab of Tony's pickup as the Rivas's returned to San Xavier. Danny sat beside Sophie in the rear, lost in private reflection of the day's events. With his head resting against the open window frame, he let the wind clip his hair and bathe his face in its warmth. The fragrant smell of purple sage filled his lungs while a forest of odd-shaped saguaros zipped by.

He hoped the warm feeling inside would last. It felt invigorating; exactly what he'd need for the challenges ahead. Several days of work at Kitt Peak and the project for Mr. Jensen seemed pretty scary. If only he could concentrate on the things Joseph had said; like the fact that Coyote was with him, then he was sure he would succeed.

Danny sat by Jensen's desk anxiously watching Alex Winterbottom in the chair next to him. He wasn't sure how Alex felt, but as far as he was concerned the waiting was just plain painful.

It was Monday afternoon and they were about to leave for Kitt Peak and the start of their first full week at the observatory. But before they went Jensen had asked to speak with them about how Thursday and Friday had gone. Dr. Richards had sent an early report and they now waited for Jensen to return from the teacher's room to share the details.

"What are you thinking?" asked Alex, his fingers drumming the desktop.

"I'm not thinking of much right now," Danny quaked, "because if I do I might pee my pants."

"Yes, well, it has been determined that excessive stress experienced over long periods can cause a synaptic gap in the brain affecting the function of the urinary tract."

"Huh?"

Alex pushed on the nosepiece of his glasses. "Basically, it's a downhill flow with no shutoff."

Suddenly, the door swung open and in walked Jensen with a smile on his face and a manila folder tucked under his arm. He spun his chair around, straddling it backwards.

"So, guys, how are you feeling about the first days of your experience?" He studied each of them carefully.

Danny couldn't keep it in. "It's been great, Mr. Jensen. Dr. Richards is awesome and so are the telescopes. I mean, I've learned a ton of stuff already."

"Y-Yes, he's right..." Alex nodded dumbly.

"Feeling good? Excellent, because that's how Dr. Richards sees it, too. In fact, he says in his report that you've had an outstanding start, particularly in your understanding of some pretty complex systems." He swatted his desk with the rolled-up folder. "I'm proud of you both, very proud...and so is San Xavier School."

"Whoa," gleamed Danny.

"Whoa is right," Jensen said. "Now, have you been thinking of possible topics for your class presentations?"

"Um, if Alex doesn't mind, I'd like to do mine on the constellation Virgo. That's the star group we watched on Friday."

"That's fine. What about you, Alex?"

"I was thinking of a model of the Mayall reflector, sir."

Jensen nodded, "those are both terrific ideas. Okay, you'll do your presenting in class a week from Wednesday. Do you have any other questions?"

Danny stared back; too excited to speak. What news he had! He couldn't wait to tell everyone. If Joseph didn't call tonight, he'd call him first thing in the morning.

As they boarded the minibus for the trip to the observatory, he thought about what Tony had said at the picnic. It was the first time he ever remembered him actually revealing what was in his heart. And it felt good to Danny, but he knew actions counted more than words. The next few weeks would probably tell.

With his mind in a jumble he barely noticed the stiff seat and bumpy ride; a far cry from the comfort of Joseph's old Ford.

He listened to the sound of the engine, trying to calm himself before they reached the station. All he could do now, he decided, was practice what to say and hope for the best.

He clutched the phone to his ear, smiling broadly as he listened to Joseph sing a froggy version of the waila song from the picnic.

"You're like that Willie guy with the red bandana. Right, Willie Nelson. Y-Yeah, I had a great time on Sunday. So did everybody. Hey, what do you think of this? I got an excellent report from Dr. Richards up at Kitt Peak. That place is awesome and I've learned a lot."

He waited for Joseph to finish praising.

"Thanks. Anyway, I'm giving a presentation to the class in a week or so and I was wondering if you'd come. Um, Mr. Jensen just called to say the principal, Father Dobson, will be there and I could invite whoever I want. Dad said he'd try to find time from work..." He covered his mouth quickly. "So, what else is new?"

A guilty look began to creep across his face as he paused for Joseph's rapid response.

"Yes, I know. I need to be more patient on the good, red road. Sorry, Grandfather. But Mom is coming..."

His expression turned to joy. Dropping cross-legged to the floor, he scratched his back anxiously against the door frame.

"You will? Cool beans!"

He shook his head at Joseph's vague reply.

"Uh, no, beans can be cool, Grandfather."

"Yup, right, it's a Wednesday at one o'clock in room two hundred. It's just down the hall from the gym doors. Great, I'll see you then."

His mind was a blur—Kitt Peak, star systems, standing in front of the class—the important thing to worry about now was the presentation. Would Mr. Jensen and Father Dobson be impressed? How about the other kids? What if no one liked it? He tried to push that last thought from his mind.

"Come on, Coyote-meeter," he muttered, "you can do it."

As their assignment with Dr. Richards at Kitt Peak entered its last days, Danny started to understand what Tony meant by a tight work schedule. How was he ever going to finish his project for Wednesday?

He had decided on a folding storyboard with constellation Virgo set in the center as a three-dimensional model. Positioned around the board would be written descriptions of each star in the group. He would type them up one at a time and print them out on a school computer during study hall.

It sure sounded like a good plan, but when it came to actually putting together the model he hit a serious snag. The stars in the system were so far apart—measured in space miles—that he couldn't calculate the scale correctly. They ended up spread out like bobbers on a fishing line or clumped together like bunches of grapes. Either way, it looked goofy. With determination in his eyes, he pulled out his graphing calculator.

After several tries using strange combinations of wire, glue, styrofoam balls, star stickers, and pipe cleaners, he finally came up with something quite eye-catching, he thought. He stood in the back of the art room admiring his completed model. The fake stars shimmered at the ends of gently jiggling strands of wire—all lined up like dominoes ready for spontaneous collapse if anyone got too close and careless.

He decided that the best part was opening the bifold and watching the whole constellation spring out like a pop-up book. Well, if it wasn't worthy of the Albert Einstein Award, it was definitely good enough to impress Mr. Jensen and the class.

He placed all of his materials inside a portfolio and stashed it safely beneath the back counter in the lab. Turning to leave, he noticed a silvery model of the Mayall projector sitting proudly on the shelf.

"Hmm, interesting, looks like Alex has been busy, too."

Tossing his calculator and pencil onto the desk, he headed for the classroom door and the last serving in the lunchroom.

"I'll practice my speech on Theresa," he whispered. "She'll tell me how good it really is."

18

Wednesday was upon them and the time for Danny's and Alex's presentations had arrived. Their assignment at Kitt Peak had concluded the day before with both receiving a rousing endorsement from Dr. Richards. Danny found himself presenting first after losing to Alex two out of three at 'rock, paper, scissors.' It seemed Winterbottom also had telepathic powers stored in that huge brain of his.

No wonder he got perfect scores on all his math papers, thought Danny, *he could basically read minds!*

Staring out at a sea of faces, he quickly rehearsed the details of his presentation. Everything would go fine, he figured, as long as he didn't freak and forget his name. Seeing Alex's gleaming model on the table next to him didn't help, but he pushed it out of his mind and concentrated on the points he'd learned from Dr. Richards. The good news was Mr. Jensen's last minute instruction to keep it short. Now he waited patiently for the cue to begin.

"...and so I'd like to present our two San Xavier students and their projects from Kitt Peak Observatory. First, Danny Rivas and a fascinating look at the constellation Virgo."

Danny launched happily into his routine only to discover that his normal voice had disappeared, replaced by a high-pitched squeak.

"Um, t-thank..." He tried desperately to calm his thumping heart as it bounced around his chest like a ping-pong ball. "Hhhummahummm"

"That's fine, Danny," Jensen smiled. "Uh, take your time..."

"The constellation Virgo...as you can see in my diagram, is a group of distant stars which cannot be observed with the na-na-naked eye." He glanced about amid a chorus of giggles.

"Class...please," sounded Jensen.

"B-Because it's spring, Virgo is visible in the Northern Hemisphere using the four-meter Mayall projector. It's the second largest constellation in the sky, next to Hydra. W-What I think is most interesting about these stars is that they're about three hundred light years from Earth. That means their light... which is just reaching us now, started in our direction at the time of the dinosaurs, or about sixty million years ago."

Now things are starting to cook, he thought. His confidence grew even more when he spotted Digs and Theresa sitting near the front. They nodded when he spoke and seemed to be showing a keen interest.

"There are more than two thousand galaxies in Virgo."

"And didn't you observe the brightest of these?" Jensen asked suddenly.

"Yes, we did," Danny replied. "It's called the Sombrero Galaxy because it has dust around its equator, making it look like a hat...a sombrero."

"That's really outstanding work, please continue."

"Okay, great, um..."

Just then, a bustle of activity near the door attracted their attention. Entering the room and standing in the back were the school principal, Father Dobson, Cecilia; sporting her favorite white shawl, and Joseph; dressed in a starchy shirt and turquoise string tie. This had to be special, thought Danny, since he'd never seen Joseph in anything formal before. He watched him glance about the room uncomfortably.

"Connie and Alicia," Jensen called, "would you get chairs please for our guests."

Danny waited in excitement for the class to settle. They were here just in time to watch his demonstration and listen to the grand finale—a cassette recording of a song about Spica, the brightest of the stars.

"So, to conclude my presentation I'd like to use this chart and model to demonstrate the relationship between Spica, the Big Dipper, and the Milky Way."

He glanced nervously at Joseph, sitting bent in his chair, his eyebrows scrunched in total concentration.

"As you can see, Spica is located here...just above the handle of the Big Dipper and a great distance from the Milky Way... which is back here." He pointed carefully at his model.

"Even so, the Milky Way is still a member of the same group of galaxies. Now, if I connect this wire to my battery pack..."

He smiled as small Styrofoam globes began to rotate.

"...I can show the spiral movement of the stars. And when I attach this second wire...like this...the others move elliptically."

He beamed as a spattering of applause broke out in the room. Mr. Jensen seemed to clap the loudest.

"Danny, that's terrific," he called above the noise. "Verrrry impressive."

His spirit soaring, Danny searched the faces in the room. There was Theresa, smiling at him from her chair. An exclamation of "Yea, Danny!" burst from her mouth. Beside her, Joseph began to clap in unison with the others. Digs hooted at him from the second row while Theresa waved and cheered. Even Alex Winterbottom was applauding, although his concentration was beginning to shift to his model on the table as he prepared to take his turn.

What a cool feeling, he thought. *They liked it. They're actually showing their appreciation—and to a 'dumb little punk' like me. I guess I'm not so dumb. And maybe Coyote has a hand in this too.*

He basked in the glow. This was more than he could have imagined possible just a few short weeks ago. He was feeling wanted—special, and all the students in the class were accepting him for who he was; the real Danny Rivas, not some lame excuse for a runaway.

While the applause began to dwindle in the crowd, one source of clapping continued from the back stronger than ever. It was Joseph, so overwhelmed with emotion that he'd lost track of the others. He continued to cheer and stamp his feet even after Cecilia signaled him with a stiff tug on his shirtsleeve.

Danny pushed the play button on the recorder, filling the room with the heavenly sounds of "Spica, the White-Blue Star."

While the class listened to the music, he gathered his materials and signaled Mr. Jensen that he was finished.

Danny's grounding ended that Friday and he was determined to catch up on things with Digs Ramirez. They hadn't seen much of each other since he and Joseph had returned from the desert.

He longed to let loose a little and get his mind off school for a change. Sure, the science project had turned out better than he could have predicted and Cecilia, Tony, and Joseph had praised him up and down, but he had reached the point of overload; a feeling that was tough to describe and even tougher to shake off. He was all in a daze with nothing in particular staying in his mind for long. A day away from random thoughts of parallel universes and spiral star movements would do his heart good.

Dawn on Saturday had barely broken over the eastern ridges of the Rincon Mountains when he and Digs found themselves well along the trail into Little Wild Horse Canyon. They'd brought along a backpack stuffed with extra clothes and plenty of Cecilia's tortillas wrapped in tin foil. With any luck, and some help from early monsoons, there would still be water flowing in the creek below Helmet Peak. And a current in the creek meant water over the falls at Apache Eye Basin where a deep pool waited.

They joked along the way, making up stories about Jake and Eddie. Nick and Sister Margarite were fair game too. But when Digs raved about the dress with spaghetti straps he'd seen Theresa wearing in San Xavier Plaza, Danny's jealous frown told him to change the subject.

As they approached within earshot of the basin they detected the splash of water against rocks and a more distant roar from the falls. There would indeed be enough water for swimming! Winding their way among giant boulders to the base of the falls, they pulled two pair of cut-off jeans from the pack and were soon dog-paddling about in the cold depths.

They took turns challenging one another to feats of skill, like who could swim underwater the farthest or who could shoot the straightest by knocking a plastic water bottle off a rock at thirty feet (Digs won, striking the bottle four times in a row and collecting a quarter for each direct hit).

Danny couldn't remember when he'd had more fun. It was one of those afternoons he wouldn't trade for a million quarters. He held out until the sun dipped below the trees before suggesting to Digs that they start back.

But it was at the start of a new school week and just as homeroom was ending that the pace picked up again. Mr. Jensen had taken attendance and two students from Sister Margarite's class had led the school in the Pledge of Allegiance when Danny was quietly called to the teacher's desk. He tried to make something of Jensen's waxy smile as he approached, but quickly remembered how deceiving looks could be.

"Okay, you folks are dismissed," voiced Jensen. "Let's get to first mod quickly please. Thanks."

"You wanted to see me, sir?"

"Yes, I had a chance to evaluate your project over the weekend and I must say you certainly did your research and knew your subject matter very well. Based on all the indicators, along with reports from Dr. Richards, you will receive an 'A plus.' This is not a grade I often award to a student," he said, reaching to shake his hand. "Congratulations and..."

"A-And what?" Danny stammered.

"I have an opportunity in mind that I'd like you to seriously consider."

"Opportunity?"

"I know this is a lot for you to hear all at once, but I'm referring to a chance for you to attend the De Massey Academy in Denver, possibly this coming fall."

His head started to buzz. "D-Denver...Colorado, but why?"

"Well, because it's my opinion, and that of Dr. Richards, that you could really excel in mathematics and the sciences given the right environment. That is, if you are willing to push yourself more than you ever have before."

"How can I...I mean, where would I live and stuff?"

"If you are accepted, the total cost would be paid by a grant from the National Science Foundation. It's a government scholarship program for those who meet entrance requirements. You would be housed on campus at their Denver facility with room and board paid by the taxpayers."

"Mom and Dad...and Joseph wouldn't..."

Jensen sat forward in his chair. "You see, Danny, in spite of all that's been said about America being the great land of opportunity and a world leader...uh, those things are true, by the way...the fact remains we're in a fight to maintain our leadership role. Asian countries like China, Japan, and Korea are advancing rapidly and competing fiercely in a global economy. And the key to victory is knowledge...advances in technology. To put it more simply, we need a highly trained, skilled workforce, particularly in the fields of math and science."

Danny blinked numbly. "B-But I'm O'odham and I l-live here...in the desert...on the reservation. Everything in my life is here...G-Grandfather and my friends, Digs and Theresa." Tears welled in his eyes. "I don't think this is a good idea, Mr. Jensen. Really, I-I..."

"I'm sorry; maybe I should have given you this in smaller bits. It's just that I believe you are gifted, and I know you love the subject matter too." He moved from behind the desk. "You're proud to be O'odham, aren't you?"

"W-Well, yeah, I am."

"Then from now on I want you to outwardly express that pride. Don't you see? Your heritage doesn't limit your horizons or lessen your chances. It increases them, a thousand times over." He got in Danny's face. "See my eyes? Come on, look. Do they seem clouded to you?"

"I-I, no, they don't, but."

"You know, I didn't give up on the idea of becoming a teacher because my family had no money to help me with college. My great-grandfather was a farmer and came here from Denmark without a penny to his name."

"It's not really the same for us, Mr. Jensen," he sniffed. "We had our land taken from…"

"And my great-grandfather didn't? Poverty took his land, Danny, along with crop failure and an upper class that squeezed the life from him."

"Please, sir," he choked, "I'm sure…it's just that I think I really need to talk it over with my family, you know?"

Jensen placed a hand on his shoulder. "I apologize for lecturing you or saying anything offensive. I certainly hope I didn't. I can get carried away when it comes to thinking of possibilities for my students. Yes, I *do* understand how you're feeling. There are others to consider. Would you like me to approach your family with this? I can help if you want."

The sincerity in his voice made Danny feel calmer. He searched Jensen's eyes for an answer, only to realize it would need to come from his own heart.

"I'd like to talk it over with my grandfather, if that's okay."

"Sure thing and I'm right here if you need me," Jensen replied.

Danny suddenly found himself at his locker down the hall, but try as he might, he couldn't remember leaving Jensen's room.

19

Danny thought of little else except Mr. Jensen's proposal in the days ahead. And what had started out sounding like something way beyond his reach (in fact, almost too ridiculous to mention) had gradually become an idea that appealed to him.

Denver wasn't so far away that he couldn't come home once in a while. Sure, he'd miss his friends, but this was an opportunity to make new ones and learn about the world outside of San Xavier. As it was, he'd visited Tucson with his class to see a stage production at the Fox Theatre and been on a science field trip to view the mineral collection at the University of Arizona. He knew that big cities offered a whole lot of interesting and exciting things to do.

After some long hard thinking, he'd figured out a way to bring up the subject with his family. He wouldn't call on Mr. Jensen just yet. That would make him look needy; like he didn't care enough to try it on his own first. And Jensen might come off as an outsider, especially with Tony and Joseph who tended to be wary of strangers. Better to get Cecilia alone first, and away from a possible quick reaction from the others. And that was where Joseph would come in.

Danny knew his grandfather would be his best chance, in spite of the fact that Joseph didn't understand math or science and seemed out of place at school. He was way smart at other things, like seeing what was in a person's heart—Danny's heart. He was a leader among the Tohono O'odham and people respected him. Danny remembered how the store clerk had reacted. He also knew Cecilia would listen. She loved her father—just as much as he did.

By the time the bell sounded from the school tower on Friday afternoon, he felt he'd waited long enough. It was time for action and Mr. Jensen needed an answer.

He and Cecilia were going to Sells in the morning to shop at the farmer's market and take fresh poblanos and tomatoes over to Joseph and Delores in Pan Tak. As they often did on such weekend visits, Danny and his grandfather would walk along the trail that ringed the village in search of bits of copper and quartz for his medicine pouch. Joseph would be at his best, for this was a task he truly loved. A good time and place, Danny thought, to mention the academy in Denver.

Leaning heavily on his walking stick, Joseph stooped to pull the half-buried rock from the sand. He studied the bottom of the stone carefully, looking for blue-green traces of copper.

"Be alert, my son, for nakshel, the scorpion. He hides from the sun and does not like it when his roof is torn off. He will sting first and ask questions later."

"Yes, you warned me the last time, Grandfather," Danny answered. "Don't you remember?"

"What I remember is a time in the old days when we would dam up the water in a trench to grow our corn. My father left me to watch over the dam and keep the water from leaking out. If it did he got mad and hollered from the field...'Joseph, are you sleeping?!' Sometimes I was, but it was usually too late to do anything about it because the water had already drained away. In the same way, there is much that leaves my mind now and does not return. I'm afraid the dam is leaking again."

A cottontail skittered from their path as they continued along the desert track. Danny kept a steady eye on Joseph who kept an even keener eye on the ground in front of them.

"So, what do you think about the scholarship and De Massey Academy? I was kind of hoping you'd help me talk to Mom and Dad about it."

"I don't know how to answer you," he sighed. "It is true that if I speak with Cecilia she will listen, but you have cut me to the quick and I can only ask questions. It is such a big decision to make."

He could sense Joseph hedging. "Um, yeah, and I'm sorry to spring it on you l-like this, but Mr. Jensen sort of did the same thing to me."

Joseph coughed to clear his throat. "I will walk with you until my last step on Mother Earth...this you must know. But I am an old man and I see in ways of the past. I am happy to talk to your mother if you want, for I should not interfere with what your heart tells you to do."

"No, please, Grandfather," he pleaded, grabbing his sleeve. "You're the smartest person in the world and I trust you more than anyone. That's just it...San Xavier is my home, and the desert too...especially the desert. I don't know what to do. I'm confused."

"Then maybe we should know for sure before I go to Cecilia about this new school. It sounds like you want to go and you don't want to go. It also makes me wonder about Coyote. Do you remember his calling and are you listening carefully to what he is saying?"

"I've tried...really, I have. But sometimes I don't understand what he wants of me."

"As I have said, he wants you to look at your reflection to find truth. And when you see yourself, do you see something missing? Are you forgetting about what's important?"

Danny sighed deeply. "Maybe he thinks I should try harder?"

"Well, this you have done and I am proud of you. But maybe there is more to accomplish and you should journey to find a sign, yes?"

"Do you think he'll tell me that I should go to school in Colorado?"

"Hmm, perhaps, or that your true path will return you to the land of your people," said Joseph. "That I cannot say, but if you seek him out you may come to know."

"Then that's it," declared Danny. "But uh, where should I look?"

"It will not be an easy thing. Coyote keeps many homes in the desert and does not stay anywhere for long. But there is one place where it is said he meets with Elder Brother. If we travel there we might find your answer."

"Where? What place are you talking about?"

"The cave of I'itoi and birthplace of all mankind… Baboquivari."

"Baboquivari," he repeated mysteriously. "We learned about the mountain in third grade. Are we going to climb up there? Isn't it considered sacred ground?"

Joseph smiled, "the cave is near the summit and yes, it is sacred, but no O'odham should ever fear walking there. It has been many years since my last visit. The climb may be too difficult for me, but I will not know until I try."

"Isn't it a long way from here?"

"It is too far for us to walk from San Xavier, but not from the village of Pitoikam," he said. "The White Shadow knows the way to an elder's house near the trailhead. I know of ancient canyon paths to reach the cave. They are steep with giant boulders and it's easy to become lost, but I still remember. There is a hidden spring with fresh water along the way. We could make the journey in two days if we do not stop to talk to the birds."

Danny stared with wide-eyed enthusiasm. "Do you think we should?

"The light in your eyes gives me courage…while a man my age should know better. On the other hand, a life that is not lived is empty."

"Yeah, that's right, Grandfather," he chirped. "Let's go…I know we can make it."

Joseph stared down with loving eyes. "It is settled then," he finally said. "But we cannot tell the others of our true plan. It must look like we are camping at Sheep's Head Rock instead."

"To Baboquivari," Danny grinned.

"To Baboquivari, my son," nodded the old man.

Part Three

The Journey

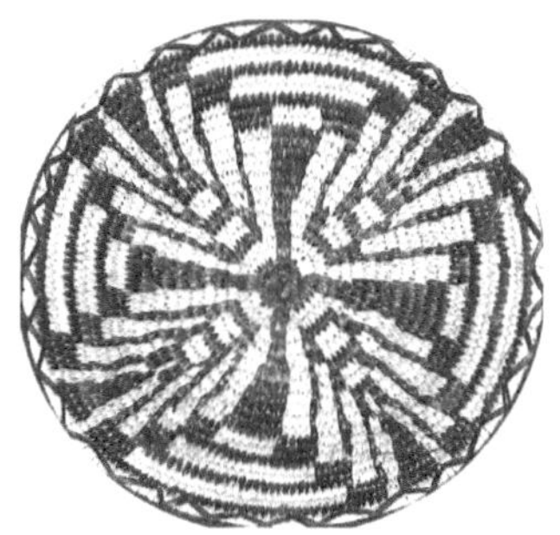

20

"Are you ready for this?" Danny bubbled.

"Whaa naa?" mumbled Digs Ramirez, his mouth crammed with hoagie roll and turkey loaf. A bead of mayonnaise oozed down his chin.

"Eat much?"

Digs worked hard to swallow the food. "Why not, is what I said. Hey, I didn't have breakfast. It was either food or the bus. Some choice, huh? Because if I'd missed the bus then why would I have bothered to get up in the first place, ya know?"

"Brilliant, just brilliant."

"What can I say?" he shirked, "I try." He took another dive into the fat sandwich.

"I would only share this with you," whispered Danny, eyeing two girls sitting an arm's length down the table. "So, not a soul, got it?"

"Sure, what's up?"

"Ever hear of Baboquivari?"

"Babble, what?"

"Bab...Hmm, I guess that's my answer."

"Listen, genius," he piped, "just because your science project was a hit, don't forget that you totally suck in language arts. The entire class would sign a petition kicking you out if they could."

"Come on, not so loud," whispered Danny nervously. "Anyway, it's a mountain on the reservation...sacred to my people. According to O'odham belief, it's where man was born. There's a cave near the top where I'itoi, Elder Brother, first emerged to walk on the land. And I'm going up there this coming weekend."

"Really? Cool, got room for me?"

"Afraid not, Digs, I'm going with Joseph. Um, we're leaving after school on Friday."

"Joseph? Man, you must be joking. You're going to climb a mountain with your grandfather? Isn't he like a hundred or something?"

"He's eighty...and what difference does it make? My grandfather could survive in the desert for a month if he wanted to."

"Well, maybe so, but climbing up a mountain is more like running fifty laps around the soccer field. Could he do that?"

Danny winced. "Okay, so we'll have to take it slow, but I really need to do this...it's about Coyote."

"Hmm, yeah I thought I might hear his name mentioned again." He peered across the table. "What's the rest of the story, muchacho?"

"Well, Mr. Jensen wants me to go to school up in Denver to study science and..."

"Denver?" Digs choked. "When were you planning to let me in on that one?"

"I'm sorry, I-I didn't exactly know how to...Aw, Digs, I'm real sorry. It's just that my parents would probably never let me go. So, I figured maybe Joseph could help convince them."

"You mean this is all basically his idea to go wandering off in the desert?"

"Uh, no, actually it was my...well, yes, maybe it was..."

"You sound very confused, mi amigo. Are you sure you don't want some extra company along for the ride? Things might get dangerous out there, especially at night."

"No, I can't, Digs. We have to do this alone. There's a lot at stake and...y-you know about Coyote's message to me." Danny watched the expression on his face. "Joseph says we'll find answers if we seek them out."

"Yeah," he nodded, "and that's pretty much out of my league. So, how long do you think it'll take?"

"We're going to shoot for a Sunday afternoon return, if all goes well." He drummed the table nervously. "As far as my parents know, Joseph and I are going to the kih at Sheep's Head Rock for a two-nighter."

Digs scratched his neck thoughtfully. "I don't know, Danny. This all sounds pretty risky to me. If something goes wrong you'll be totally on your own and not in the place where people expect you to be."

"But you'll know, Digs, right?"

"Uh, yes, I guess I will," he answered uneasily.

By the time Friday afternoon rolled around, Danny was jumping out of his shoes with excitement. He had waited nearly thirty minutes by the double doors to the school parking lot for a glimpse of Joseph driving the White Shadow. The now familiar rumble of a broken exhaust pipe would announce his arrival. And then suddenly there he was, making a wide turn toward the sidewalk. Danny ran alongside the open window exchanging eager smiles with his grandfather.

"I like what you wore to school today," said Joseph, applying the brakes. "Jeans, a couple shirts, plus a jacket ...and your hikers."

"You've always told me to layer when out in the desert."

"That I have and you listen well. I brought along an extra pair of gloves too. You know how cold it can get out there at night. Do you remember this?" he asked, tossing out a baseball cap.

Danny grinned at the sight of the faded blue hat with the curled visor—the word 'CATS' embroidered across the front in red, white, and blue block letters.

"My Arizona hat," he chirped, "so that's where it was. I swear I searched my closet three times. It's my lucky hat. Thanks, Grandfather."

"You left it behind when we drove to the picnic. Hop in, we're ready to go. I've got our gear stowed in the back and a whole knapsack full of energy food."

"I hope we didn't forget anything else."

"Nothing that I could think of...except what we'd like to forget," he added. "Uh, I'm speaking of the tall tale we told Cecilia and Tony."

"Yeah, I know," said Danny, "but it's the right thing we're doing, isn't it? I mean, we've got stuff to figure out and you said this was the best way."

"Yes, I did, and I believe this is very good medicine. Elder Brother is 'chekaidkam,' my son: 'one who can hear,' and he will show us the right path."

"Well, I sure hope it stays a secret path."

Joseph rubbed his forehead thoughtfully. "If Delores found out, she would probably say 'good enough, you old coot,' but I'm not sure about Cecilia...she'd yell a lot, I think."

"Why are they so different? I mean, Grandmother never worries and she doesn't get upset when I say or do stuff."

"Huh, she is worried out! She doesn't always approve, but leaves it for Cecilia or announces it to me sometimes. It is only because she loves you very much." He went silent for a spell. "You know, I think they are mostly different because of the times in which they grew up. Cecilia may be my daughter, but she is your mother first. You are closest to her and that changes everything. Do you see?"

"Yeah, I guess. Anyhow, they won't find out and we'll be back by Sunday." He began turning the dial on the FM radio. A series of deep thuds exploded from the speakers.

"What is that awful sound? Oooh, change it," Joseph begged.

"It's Ludacris, Grandfather. Come on," he urged, bobbing his head rhythmically, "like you said, it's the times. Be easy."

"I'm afraid there is nothing easy about listening to that."

The heavy base boomed out the window, invading the silence of the desert. Joseph swung the car onto Old Ajo Way and slowly accelerated.

Less than an hour later they had abandoned the main highway and were following a dusty trace toward the village of Pitoikam. Joseph's eyes searched the roadside for a cutoff that led to the Baboquivari trailhead.

"I've never been to this place before," Danny breathed, peering out at thick tangles of chain cholla. "We must be just about there, huh?"

"Yes, and we'll be hitting the trail just as soon as we park the car. I'd like to reach the spring below Lion's Ledge by dark. We can camp there for the night."

"Lion's Ledge...it sounds dangerous."

"It is good for hiding, that's for sure. There, the mountainside is thick with black oaks and huge boulders. The danger is in being alone, but we will have each other. That is fortunate for two travelers to such a wild place, very fortunate indeed. We must cross Lion's ledge to reach the summit. It is mountain lion country and we will see scat along the way. Perhaps, even Mawid himself."

"Scat? Yuck, more like big cat poops."

"The droppings are a warning to other lions in the area, especially young males searching for a mate of their own. Another lion's smell says stay away."

"Or prepare for battle, right?"

Joseph's eyes lit up. "That is right...and here is the cutoff. Are you ready?"

"Yup, let's go, Grandfather. It's time for Coyote-meeter to check out this Lion's Ledge place." He smiled eagerly as the car ground to a halt.

"You will see it soon enough, my son."

While Danny busied himself with the gear in the trunk, Joseph tried to prepare himself mentally. He gazed beyond the palo verdes at the dark distant outline of Baboquivari Peak.

The mountain's summit was shrouded in a deep purple cloudbank. It would be cold and windy at the cave of I'itoi. Would those winds carry the voice of Coyote to them? Only by safely passing through the steep and rugged country ahead would their hope of hearing his message be realized.

Breathing the cool sweetness of the desert into his lungs, Joseph turned to make a final check of the car. Satisfied that all was ready, he joined Danny along a faint footpath winding into the brush. Seconds later, the dark shadows had swallowed them up.

21

With a hand resting on Danny's shoulder, Joseph peered ahead into the gathering shadows of mountain cactus.

"We must keep a steady pace or we will not reach the spring by nightfall," he urged, reaching out with the tip of his walking stick.

"Don't worry, Grandfather, we've hiked in the desert before. Do you remember our last trip to the kih?"

"This will be more difficult, my son, for I see the path is little used since my last journey here and the distance we must travel is greater."

They zigzagged up the spine of a steep ridge, emerging once again into the bright rays of the sun. Nearly an hour had passed since they parked the car and struck out on the trail, yet they had advanced only half a mile through the dense Sonoran undergrowth.

"I do feel kind of out of shape," puffed Danny. "How about you?"

"I am breathing...that is what matters," Joseph answered. "Do not forget the altitude here. We are already higher than the cliffs above Sheep's Head Rock. And be listening near the ground for the sound of Ko'owi's warning."

"Grandfather, did you know rattlesnakes don't always inject venom when they bite? We learned that in Mrs. Duttweiler's class last year."

"Well, nothing personal against your teacher, Danny. I'm sure she is wise in her ways, but I will not give Ko'owi the opportunity to decide, if I can help it."

"That's what I think, too," Danny nodded. "You should come teach us at school. You're real smart about the desert and stuff."

"Hmm, I will leave that in the hands of..."

The sharp thwack of a hatchet against hardwood echoed from a stand of trees in the ravine ahead. They heard voices mix with the chopping and spotted a thin wisp of gray smoke rising from the hidden glen.

Joseph grabbed Danny's arm and they knelt quickly beside a boulder. There, they waited in silence, listening for sounds along the trail. An anxious minute passed before Joseph was sure they had not been spotted.

"I have a bad feeling about this," he whispered.

"Why, Grandfather?"

"No one among the O'odham would build a fire in such a place. The desert has gone long without rain and it is far too dangerous to do so. I fear whoever is there is foolish and does not care about our land."

"Then, who could...illegals," Danny breathed.

"Maybe so, but we cannot be sure without getting closer," he noted softly. "If we leave the trail and keep low I think we can reach those rocks by their camp. We'll be able to hear their voices clearly."

"What if they see us? We'll be dead meat."

He patted Danny's shoulder. "Sneaking into the country does not make a person dangerous, but we will try to avoid being seen. Quietly now...let's go."

They took light steps among the thorns, making sure to avoid dry sticks and debris that might snap under their weight. With slow and careful maneuvering, they made their way down the bank of the ravine, reaching the safety of the rock pile. Huddled under a jutting tooth of granite, they listened to a chorus of foreign voices arguing a short distance away. A husky cry rose above the rest.

"¡Silencio! ¡Todo usted, se sienta! He oido bastante."

Danny's eyes widened. "They *are* illegals, Grandfather. You can speak Spanish," he whispered. "What are they saying?"

"He sounds like the boss and he is very angry. He has ordered the rest to stop talking and listen." Joseph put a finger to Danny's lips. "We should not talk, either. I will hear what they say and tell you later."

"Yo no cuido si usted tiene hambre, tenemos una entrega importante para hacer."

Joseph couldn't hide his look of fear as he peered through the thicket. Leaning forward, he separated the branches for a better view.

The man in charge was stocky with wide, muscular shoulders and wearing a camouflage pattern outfit. His pants were tucked neatly into combat-style boots. Around his waist a holster belt bristled with cartridges and the grip of a steel-gray revolver waited just below his fingertips.

He pointed confidently at three, tightly wrapped cardboard boxes stacked in front of him. As he spoke his voice grew cocky and abusive.

"Este material vale más que su vive..."

A sharp point of a rock stabbed at Danny's thigh as he waited patiently for Joseph. He winced painfully, shifting his weight to relieve the pressure. Suddenly, a piece of the ledge broke free and tumbled into the ditch, landing with a thump!

A man sitting with his back to them whirled about in alarm. "¿Qué era eso?"

The air hung thick and silent about the clearing. All eyes were riveted on the very spot where Joseph and Danny lay hiding!

"Rapido...averigüelo," ordered the boss, jerking his thumb in the direction of the boulder.

Just then, a young cottontail, frightened by the man's approach, broke out of the underbrush and scampered through the camp—around and under the raised feet of the surprised immigrants. They howled and hooted with glee as the animal made its escape past the campfire and under a sprawling prickly pear.

"Sólo un conejo, el jefe," said the man, holding his index fingers against his ears to lengthen them. The group laughed nervously at his antics.

"Tipos duros...¿eh?" the boss taunted. "Descanse ahora, salimos por la mañana."

With a spattering of grumbles the men rose from their seats and moved toward a pair of pup tents pitched in the back of the clearing. The boss watched them closely; his boot perched on the stack of boxes.

Joseph and Danny inched cautiously back from their hiding spot. When they had retreated a safe distance up the slope they plunked wearily beside a palo verde to talk about what they had heard.

"They are mules," Joseph began. "They are carrying illegal drugs into the country, my son. The man with the gun is very dangerous. I believe he would stop at nothing to get his money." Breathing heavily, he rested his aged body against the tree. "The other men wanted food, but he refused them, saying they had an important delivery to make. He told them the drugs were worth more than their lives..."

"Wow, we were pretty lucky that rabbit showed up," said Danny. "What would have happened if they'd caught us?"

"I do not have that answer. It is possible they only agreed to carry the drugs for the boss if he would guide them across the desert. Anyway, I'm glad we didn't have to find out."

"That's for sure. Did he say anything else?"

"Only that they should rest for the trip north in the morning, probably to Tucson."

Danny stared anxiously down at the camp in the trees. "What should we do now, Grandfather? They're blocking our path ahead. We'll never make it to the summit and back this weekend if we don't reach Lion's Ledge tonight."

"You are right about that," Joseph answered, "but remember, this mountain and the entire desert around has been my home for all these years...I know of a way."

"You do? Cool. So, where..."

"Let us pick up our gear and drink some water first," he suggested. "This has been too much excitement for one old man...and on the first day." He stood stiffly and motioned for Danny to follow him back along the trail. "The bad news is we must move faster now," he said, pointing at a jagged peak rising above them. "Our new path will lead us over that."

"Whoa," Danny voiced. "You're kidding, right?"

"I am a healer, not a joker," assured Joseph.

"Come on, I think it's dumb, too," Digs Ramirez responded with a shake of his head.

Theresa Cerona glared at him across the snack aisle at the San Xavier Market. "I can't believe they went out there. Why didn't you stop him? I mean, you're supposed to be his best friend and all..."

"So, cut me some slack, will ya? I'm not even supposed to be telling anybody this, but I figured you'd want to know."

"Oh, great," she huffed, "and now all I do is worry my self sick. I'm serious, Digs, you get the pinhead award."

He moved closer. "Hey, what was I going to do? He was determined. You know how close he is with his grandfather...It's like they have this bond."

"And that bond will lead them both off the edge of a cliff," she frowned. "Now, tell me word for word what he said."

"Well, just that they were headed for some Babo-mountain to find the coyote Danny met in the wash." He wiped the sweat from his forehead. "You must know the story by now."

"Baboquivari?"

"Yes, that's the place. He and Joseph are looking for answers or something."

"Answers to what?"

"The thing about..." He studied her expression. "Wow, you don't know about the school in Denver, do you?"

"Wha...?"

"I'm sorry, Theresa, that I'm the one telling you this, but Mr. Jensen is trying to get Danny's family to agree to send him to a special school in Denver on a scholarship. It's some science academy, I guess." He watched her eyes sadden. "He was p-probably planning to let you know...eventually."

"Hmm, eventually," she repeated numbly.

"And, hey, he might not go," Digs offered. "I'll bet those scholarships are hard to get, you know?"

"Yes, I'm sure..."

"So, what do you think we should do?" he asked.

"I think we need to let Mrs. Rivas know right away," she said, emerging from the trance. "Climbing up Baboquivari is suicide.

They'll never make it, especially Joseph. Did he say what trail they would use?"

"No, only that they'd be gone until Sunday at the latest."

"Okay, come on." Theresa grabbed him by the hand. "There's no time to lose. In fact, we might already be too late. Danny's father will know where to look."

"I'll bet they didn't even make it to the trail," Digs declared smugly. "You've seen his grandfather's car, right? They're probably broken down out on Highway Eighty-six."

"You talk too much," she sniffed, pulling him toward the front of the store.

22

The sun nearly descended; cast a pale pink glow across the rugged features of the mountainside. Thirty-foot saguaros, rising from rocky ledges since the days of Geronimo, stood as silent sentinels guarding lost secrets of the desert.

A faint and narrow goat path, unmarked by human footprints, wound its way up the steep embankment through thickening vegetation. Only a child of Tohono; the south desert, would know of such a route to the upper reaches of Baboquivari. And yet, knowing the route was no guarantee one could safely pass over the treacherous, twisting track. That child, now in the eightieth spring of life, arm in arm with a true child of twelve, cautiously made his way among dense cactus stands that closed in around them.

"The day grows short...we are losing the light."

"Whew, this is tough climbing," Danny panted. "Are you all right, Grandfather? Maybe we should stop to drink and rest." He stared about worriedly. "I-I can't see the trail anymore."

"Yes, we should rest," Joseph sighed, dropping into a squat, "and do not fear for the trail will find us, young one."

Danny squeezed the man's arm. "I'm not really afraid...not with you. It's shaded here, let's lie down and stretch our legs."

"I will remain like this," Joseph answered, hugging his knees tightly. "It is the stance of Mo'obDam, the hunter, who tracks the wounded deer over great distance. Resting too long will cause the prey to escape or become the meal of another."

Squatting beside him, Danny pulled the water bottle from Joseph's pack and drank deeply. "Hmm, not bad. Comfortable, that is...resting like this."

Joseph smiled weakly. "Taking weight off weary legs is the sign of one who is new to the desert. Too much energy is used getting back up."

"Speaking of energy, how much farther is it to Lion's Ledge? It'll be dark soon and we left the main trail a long time ago."

"Follow the end of my finger," he said, "beyond that ridge. Do you see it in the distance? It is a flat, gray shelf of rock."

Danny peered up at the shadowy mountain. "Cool, yeah, I see it. Boy, that's still pretty far away. It looks like a couple of miles and we're kind of low on water. I sure hope you're right about the spring up there."

Joseph pulled himself upright with the walking stick. "I have never seen Scorpion's Pool dry. Come, we are almost back to the main trail and the going will be easier."

Momentarily, they were off from their rest stop, threading their way carefully between the sharp spears of two Spanish sword plants. Danny felt himself pulling Joseph along and the weight of the man's arm on his shoulder grew heavy. It was a certain sign they were both tiring, especially Joseph.

"Why do they call it Scorpion's Pool?" asked Danny.

"It was discovered long ago that I'itoi's crawling creatures would hide from the heat of the sun by visiting the water's edge. At night they covered the sand like the prickly pear."

"And we were planning to sleep there?"

"No," Joseph assured, "we will take water and camp out on the ledge where the breezes are cooling and the gnats cannot fly."

"Good idea," Danny shuddered. "We don't need the ground moving underneath us tonight."

Skirting a steep bank, they suddenly came face-to-face with a solid wall of rock rising some twenty feet above them. The faint trace they had been following had come to an end with what seemed like no way around. Danny stood staring in disbelief; first, at the impossible barrier, and then, at Joseph.

"Ah, we meet again," sighed the old man. "I had nearly forgotten, but now it comes back..." He ran his hands over the rough volcanic stone.

"What do we do now?" Danny choked. "I don't see any..."

"Patience, my son."

Joseph carefully studied the massive slab. Tiny fires kindled in his eyes as he searched and remembered. A gnarled hand shot up. "There, do you see?"

A moment of silence passed while Danny gazed at the surface. At first, it looked like any rock, but then he spotted something unusual. Angling upward across the wall was a narrow crack—not wide enough for a foothold, but just right to grip with the fingers. Below the crack, scattered about the face, were a number of gouges and crevices, stony juts and crags.

"Hey, check it out," he beamed. "Steps...W-We can use these as steps. Uh, that is I could. What about you, Grandfather?"

The old man stared painfully at the tricky climb. "I do not know. I made it the last time, but that was on younger legs." He looked about, gently rubbing his neck. "Hmm, maybe the desert has an answer."

A short distance away a sprawling ocotillo plant swayed in the breeze. Its long, spiny spears reached high into the evening sky. Danny watched Joseph carefully studying the stems.

"I get it, we make a ladder and you climb up."

Joseph ruffled the boy's hair gently. "We do not have time for such a project, but if we use our jackknives to remove the thorns we will have a sturdy pole. By reaching down with it from the top of the wall you can help pull me up the steps. What do you think?"

"Yeah, if you hold on tight..."

"Huh, I will hang on like Coyote does in the season of no rain," grunted Joseph. "Just be sure you do the same."

Cutting loose the stoutest of the needle-covered stocks, they set to the task of trimming it smooth. Danny hacked away harmlessly at the sharp barbs with his little blade.

"Ouch!" he winced, sucking the blood from his pricked finger. "Hold your end still, will you?"

"If only you were the cactus wren you would happily hop about the thorns untouched," Joseph answered. "Do not chop, but push on the blade with your thumb...like this."

In a matter of minutes Danny found himself clinging to the crack near the top of the rock, a neatly-whittled ocotillo branch hanging from his belt loop. He poked his head over the top of the wall.

"Yup, I see the trail again," he hollered. "Okay, now it's your turn, Grandfather." He scrambled onto the ledge, turning to lower the pole. Extending his arm fully, he held the spear just out of Joseph's reach.

"I cannot grab it, Danny...I must climb first."

After testing his knees on solid ground, Joseph gripped the rock above his head and began a slow rise—one cautious foot at a time.

Danny held his breath watching the silent struggle below him. Nervous sweat broke from his brow, filling his eyes with a salty sting. The juices of fear boiled in his stomach, bubbling up in the back of his throat. He swallowed hard to force it back down. He'd never felt quite this helpless before. There, just below him, was the person he loved more than anything in the world. He turned his eyes away from the edge, concentrating on the pull of Joseph's weight against the shaft. It was all he could do to keep the ocotillo steady.

"Hang on, Grandfather," he cried, gritting his teeth and digging his knees in behind him.

"Y-Yes, my...son."

Danny gripped the staff with all of his might as it swayed and jerked beneath him. Burying his face in the dirt, he fought on in stubborn silence, not daring to look again beyond the edge. On and on, he battled. And then suddenly, without warning or cry of alarm, the ocotillo lifeline went dead in his hand!

Tony Rivas's truck engine revved as he pushed the gas peddle to the floor. Twice, since leaving the house in San Xavier, he had pulled out to pass slower cars. The two sitting beside him in the cab stared wide-eyed at the road ahead. Amid cautions to watch his speed and stay off the soft shoulder of the highway, they spoke openly about their mission to find Danny and Joseph.

"How do we know they're hiking the eastern side of the mountain?" asked Tom Charro, a long-time friend of Tony's and a veteran of the Tohono O'odham Nation Police Department.

"We don't," said Tony. "Digs, you said Danny didn't mention where, right?"

"No, nothing about that. Just that he'd hiked many times with his grandfather and they'd be gone until Sunday. I told him not to do it, sir."

"It's okay, don't beat yourself up." He hit the brake as the truck bottomed out in a dip. "I guess I should be blaming Joseph for this. He's old enough to know better." He flipped on the headlights in the gathering dusk. "Thanks to his storytelling and healing potions, they've gotten themselves in a real mess. And this late in the day…They'll be at least one night in the cold."

Tom patted his arm. "No sense in blaming anyone, Tone. Let's just get in there and get them. If we can find the car and set up camp, then maybe we can catch up to them tomorrow. We've got a few things working in our favor. I've got two jeeps out first thing in the morning to check washes on the back side of Baboquivari and Burt Delaney of the Border Patrol promised to fly through with the copter. He can spot movement and smoke."

"And let's face it, Mr. Rivas," said Digs, "Joseph's car can be seen from outer space."

"Well, we need that car tonight," Tony voiced. "Joseph's a tough old bird, but that desert is tougher. Tom, if you were hiking Baboquivari, what approach would you use?"

A long silence meant his friend was thinking. "But the question is not about me, Tone…it's about your father-in-law. Where would he be headed? Knowing that would make things a lot easier."

"I'd say the cave," murmured Tony.

"The cave of I'itoi?"

"Yeah," chimed Digs, "I'll bet you're right. Danny talked about meeting Coyote somewhere."

"Coyote-meet…huh, there goes old Joseph again," whispered Tony. "So, it's as good a shot as we can take. Our first stop then… the trailhead at Pitoikam."

The truck sped deeper into the night, carrying the rescuers past the turnoff to Kitt Peak Observatory. Before they reached

Sells, a small roadside arrow would point them toward the tiny farm village of Pitoikam.

Unaware of the plight of the two hikers, they focused all their attention on the dark landscape speeding by. If they missed the sign they would have to backtrack, losing valuable time.

"There it is!" hollered Digs.

The tires on Tony's truck skidded and squealed as he applied the brakes. A quick spin of the steering wheel and they were off the main highway, bouncing down a narrow, dusty track.

Somewhere ahead, a scattering of lights would mark the few dwellings in the settlement. As they approached the outskirts, they watched for the turn to the parking lot.

"What's the overnight low supposed to be?" asked Tony.

"TV news said forty-five to fifty," Tom answered.

"Okay, but that's in the valleys. It'll be much colder up where they are." He swore and shook his head. "That is unless they get a fire going."

"Listen, Tone, we're doing what we can for now. Come tomorrow and we get a couple breaks...everything will work out, you'll see."

"Oh baby, whataya think!" grinned Tony. "We just got our first break."

Looming out of the dark, the wide outline of Joseph's Ford had the look of an iceberg adrift in a gloomy sea. Pulling alongside, they cast the beam of a flashlight in through fog-covered windows. The glint of trade beads adorning a dream catcher reflected in their eyes. The car's interior was shadowy and silent.

"I was just hoping," Tom sighed, placing an arm on Tony's shoulder.

"Yeah, I know," he whispered, turning his gaze toward the black shape of Baboquivari.

23

"My hand...t-take it, my son," Joseph gasped.

Danny jumped at the sound close by his ear. Leaning out over the edge, he spotted the frightened face of his grandfather just a few feet from his outstretched arm! A wild look of struggle to hold on—to survive—flashed in the old man's eyes.

A sob caught in the back of Danny's throat and tears streamed down his cheeks. "Grandfather! I'm here..."

His legs churned in the loose gravel as he scrambled recklessly closer to the drop-off. Straining and reaching, he tried to grip the ends of Joseph's fingers. A slide of sand and stones poured down around the old man's shoulders as he clung to the rock.

"Stay back, Danny, or you will fall," choked Joseph. "I must... get a foothold..."

Danny watched in terrified silence as the strain in the man's face increased. And then, just as quickly, an expression of relief flooded Joseph's features. Slowly, carefully, he began to inch his way up the incline.

"Turn away and grab something solid," he breathed. "I will hang on to your legs and you can drag me up."

Danny whirled about and grasped the exposed roots of a thorn bush. Feeling a tug at his feet, he pulled as hard as he could—up, gradually up—until Joseph was safely beside him. They lay still for a time, breathless and wasted from their ordeal.

"I was well on my journey to the East," Joseph rasped. "You were very brave, young one, and would not let me leave just yet. But I feel weak and my heart is heavy."

"Please," Danny blurted, "w-we can make it, I know we can. Once we get to Lion's Ledge we'll rest up. I know how to build a good fire...a-and I can cook too."

"Yes, but we are not at the kih and we do not have the olla," he responded feebly.

"Come on, Grandfather, we don't need that stuff...really. I mean, we're a team and..." He started to cry. "You said it yourself,

I'm Coyote-meeter and we need answers, right?" His teeth chattered with emotion. "Yeah, like what's in my heart...and Dad's too. A-And the thing with Mr. Jensen...the school. It's maybe a chance for me."

The tiniest spark lit in Joseph's eye. Wrapping a weak arm around Danny's neck, he struggled to his feet.

"Come, my O'odham warrior, you will carry us both to the cave of I'itoi." He pointed at the discarded ocotillo shaft. "And I will need a new walking stick."

With staff and gear in hand, they started out once again on the rugged moonlit path. Now their progress was measured as inches—into feet; a slow, deliberate shuffle. Danny kept a tight hold around Joseph's waist as they moved. With stars filling the night sky, they finally crested the ridge and rejoined the old trail. Just above them waited Lion's ledge with the dark summit of Baboquivari visible in the background.

"Here, the last of the water," said Danny.

"Do not worry," panted Joseph, sipping gratefully from the canteen. "Scorpion's Pool is nearby. We must go there first before we camp on the ledge. I-It is not much further, my son."

"How do we find it in the dark?"

Joseph stared intently into the black shadows of the mountainside. "Up there...behind that boulder is an opening in the rocks that leads to the spring."

Advancing more quickly, they discovered the narrow alley and slipped silently in among towering walls of granite.

"Wow, this is totally hidden," Danny trumpeted, his voice echoing along the passage.

"Among the O'odham who venture here, the path is known. Its source is a secret to all others," answered Joseph. "The way becomes very tight here, but we can squeeze through."

"There's water!" cried Danny. "I can smell it...and I hear it dripping."

"Ge'e wehnag mahkigdag," chanted Joseph, "Elder Brother's gift."

Just then, a low animal growl rose in the darkness ahead: louder, deeper, fearful, and then angry—a snarl as they came within sight of the glimmering pool. Danny placed a protective hand on Joseph's shoulder.

"I know the sound, Grandfather," he whispered. "That day in the wash."

"And it is the same? You are sure?"

"I'm positive. I wouldn't forget his warning in a million years."

"Ayee, then you are truly in the hand of the Creator," he replied. "It is proof, my son."

On the far side of the spring, a large, hunched shape shrunk back against the rock wall. The creature's dark hair bristled along its spine while its crimson eyes blazed and its teeth glistened in the beam of Danny's flashlight.

"Will he attack?"

"We are in danger only if we do not leave him an escape route," explained Joseph. "And since there is no other way out, we must show him the door."

They edged slowly and carefully along the wall. No sooner had they left the spot than the coyote saw its chance and bolted for the gap, its paws barely casting a ripple on the surface of the pool. Instantly, it disappeared down the narrow trail.

"He didn't make a sound," Danny marveled.

"As silent as wind tossing the feathers of a quail," sighed Joseph. "Let us get our water and return to the ledge. I-It has been the hardest day of my life...and I must rest."

After filling their canteens, Danny led the way back along the bank to Lion's Ledge. Gripping Joseph's exhausted frame, he bore his weight out onto the huge shelf of rock. The ledge was actually a cantilever, pushed out from the cliff face by natural forces over thousands of years. In a shallow depression, he lowered Joseph and their gear.

"We need a fire to warm us, Grandfather. Here, hold my flashlight and I'll be back with wood to burn."

Gathering as many loose pieces of mesquite as he could find, he returned to create a tepee-like pile of kindling that would quickly build flame. By slowly adding pieces of dried ocotillo along with the stump of a dead oak dragged from nearby, he soon had a fire crackling in the pit. Sparks flew into the night air as they huddled close, pulling blanket rolls up around them.

"It's not much, but it'll give us energy," said Danny, reaching from his backpack with tortillas and strips of beef jerky folded in tinfoil. He noticed a tremor in Joseph's hand as he drank from the canteen and accepted the meat. "Come on, Grandfather, you've got to chew it...eat as much as you can."

For a time they managed only an occasional glance, fearing signs of defeat in the eyes of the other. When their meal was finished and the fire stoked, they lowered themselves into a worn out sleep.

Having bravely fought the mountain, avoiding danger as they moved, Danny and Joseph had made the climb to Lion's Ledge. Above them in the darkness waited the summit of Baboquivari and I'itoi's cave; still a hard day's hike away.

Twice during the night, Joseph awoke to stare fearfully at the peak of the mountain. He knew something that his grandson did not—that the passage of time since his last visit to this place of eternity had taken from him the strength of his manhood. He knew the climb ahead was steep and treacherous—and that he would not be making the journey come daybreak. Danny must scale the heights to I'itoi's cave alone.

Tony Rivas; warmly dressed with hiking boots in hand, nudged Tom Charro's arm as it hung loosely off the tailgate of the truck. Laid out side-by-side in the bed of the pickup, two sleeping figures bundled in forest plaid sleeping bags stretched and squirmed about.

"Come on, guys, it's four-thirty and time to hit the trail."

Digs Ramirez gazed zombie-eyed from inside his wrap. "Whoa, Mr. Rivas, we just gahh..." A gigantic yawn escaped his mouth. "...to sleep...aaand it's still dark out."

"Yeah, for about another half hour, but we'll manage okay with flashlights." He sat on the gate, pulling on his boots and tying the laces. "Besides, you know as well as I do that we could pay dearly for lost time today, so lets go...move your butts."

"I'll radio Burt to make sure he's got the chopper ready for first light," grunted Tom, kicking out of his bag.

In a matter of minutes, they had loaded their gear and were trudging earnestly along the same track Danny and Joseph had traveled only hours before. The tiny figure of a pygmy owl watched them pass from the safety of an overhanging branch.

Toot...toot...toot...toot...tooooot.

It seemed to wish them well on their mission. Digs eyed the little raptor curiously, tripping on a loose rock as he walked.

"Did you get through to him, Tom?" asked Tony as they topped the first ridge. He motioned for them to push on amid a sea of cholla cactus.

"I did," he puffed, suddenly digging in his backpack. "We should hear the rotors soon. I'll use this tee shirt to signal him. It's important that he know our location so he can spot the trail."

Tony peered at the eastern horizon. "Good, because we're counting on him, big time."

"It's an awfully big desert, Mr. Charro," Digs declared, hustling to catch up.

"Don't worry, Joseph's white car and our pickup will be easy for him," he assured. "He'll find us."

"Watch your water, son," Tony called, "This is a dry trail. I've heard stories of a spring, but..."

"Right, but where?" added Tom. "I'll say this...if anyone knows, it would be Joseph."

Objects began to gather form around them as an orange glow built in the early morning sky. Crossing the saddle of a boulder-strewn ridge, they worked the switchbacks up the mountainside, stopping only occasionally for water and encouragement. Soon they were among the giant saguaros, passing between fading shadows and gathering sunlight.

Out of the valley below came the drone of an aircraft engine and the thump of propellers. Turning toward the sound, the rescuers watched the approach of the A-Star 350. With spirits lifted, Tony and Digs hooted and swung their arms wildly while Tom Charro waved his cotton flag.

"What a sight," cried Tony, shielding his eyes against the swirling dust. "Now we're talking."

"He'll find them. I just know it, Mr. Rivas," Digs yelled above the roar.

From the cockpit window the pilot gazed down on the trail.

He nodded in Tom's direction, expertly maneuvering the craft for a better look at the terrain. His eyes scanned the rough landscape, looking for breaks in the undergrowth where the path might lead. The copter hovered for a time before finally lifting away in a wide arc across the face of Baboquivari.

"Boys, keep your fingers crossed that Danny and Joseph got a fire going," said Tom. "If they did, Burt will spot the smoke."

Tony nervously wiped the grime from his mouth. "And if they didn't, then they had one hell of a cold night."

As the hikers renewed their climb, Burt Delaney guided the A-Star between twin peaks of jagged rock just a few miles away. He stared excitedly into the thick vegetation below. There, rising from the vast mountain like a miracle—like some godly answer to the prayers of the world—a thin gray twist of smoke curled gracefully into the air.

24

"¡El fuego, lo moja!" the man snarled, yanking the revolver from his holster belt. Ducking his head, he scampered under the protective cover of a mesquite tree.

The camp of smugglers sprang into action as two men rushed the fire pit, scooping sand on the flame and scuffing the coals with their feet. With wild eyes searching the sky, the rest of the group scattered into the brush. They waited in the dusty shadows, peering anxiously at the figure of their boss across the clearing.

"Puesto mueve, todo usted," he barked, motioning for them to stay still. Bracing against the tree, he brought the barrel of the pistol to rest on a branch above his head.

"Hmm, puffs of smoke," frowned Delaney from the seat of the 350. "That means they've cut the fire, but why?"

He brought the aircraft about sharply, hitting the descent and hovering just above the ground. Nudging the controls gently, he closed in on the crop of trees.

It was then he spotted the stacked boxes and the tents in the back of the clearing. All about were scattered articles of clothing; a tee shirt here and a pair of shorts there.

"Uh oh, wrong camp," he groaned, "and it sure looks like they left in a hurry."

He was startled by a sudden sound of impact against the copter's glass—a single, high-pitched plink was heard inside the cockpit. He felt something graze his ear, thumping into the storage compartment behind his seat. There in the windshield, only inches to his left, was a perfect half-inch bullet hole.

"Naco Station, this is two, six, niner," he blared into the mouthpiece receiver. "Do you read, over? I have a code yellow, officer taking fire."

Pulling back hard on the control stick, he felt a twinge in the pit of his stomach as the hydraulics lifted the craft rapidly skyward. He glanced quickly at the GPS panel on the console.

"My position is thirty-one north, twenty-two minutes—one-eleven west, six minutes...I need immediate backup."

A thousand feet higher and five hundred yards to the south, Delaney locked the A-Star in a tight hover. He needed to take quick stock of the damage to the copter before deciding to abort or continue the rescue. Reaching behind his seat, he removed the storage cover to examine the spot where the bullet impacted. He had been very lucky. His steel-cased first aid kit had suffered a direct hit, but the backside was undamaged. Shaking the box vigorously, he heard the unmistakable rattle of a spent slug inside.

"It's a forty caliber, alright," he muttered, turning the lump of lead with his fingers. "Now that's a serious weapon."

Pressing the headphone against his ear, he spoke quietly into the mouthpiece. "Naco...two, six, niner reports no serious damage to the craft. We have mules on the ground at last coordinates." He squinted into the rising sun. "I'm about four miles due west of Pitoikam on the east face of Baboquivari. Can you cover, over?"

Listening to the static buzz from base command, he finally raised a clenched fist triumphantly. "That's a ten-four, I'll warn Tom Charro about these yahoos. My guess is they're on the move and you can head them off on Old Ajo Highway. I'm returning to mission, and thanks...over and out."

After making a final check of his instruments, he swung the copter away from the smuggler's camp and resumed his careful search of the ridgelines. By now, morning sun beat directly against the face of Baboquivari and valuable time had been lost in the hunt for Danny and Joseph.

"Man, what a tangle," he voiced as he studied the thick brush and jagged rock formations. "If you guys can see me, I hope you send a signal...something...anything."

The small craft droned on, viewed from afar as a white speck of hope against a wide expanse of mountain green.

Danny awoke with stiffness in his legs and the smell of charcoal on his shirt and hands. The last living embers of the fire glowed red in the bottom of the pit. It was well after sunrise and he had slept longer than planned. He stared about in search of his grandfather's familiar figure. There, at the very edge of the deep chasm, sat Joseph, his blanket pulled over his shoulders.

Rising from his bedroll, Danny made a noisy approach to avoid startling him. He heard him chanting and saw him raise an object in the air.

"It's beautiful, what is it?" he asked, sitting beside him cross-legged.

Suddenly, Joseph reached for his face, brushing him with downy feathers attached to the end of an ornately carved stick.

"I am sorry, my son, for I am humiliated, and so I must do this, even though you do not possess eagle power."

"I-I don't have eagle...what?" Danny sputtered.

"The great bird's strength belongs only to those who have collected many downy breast feathers to fill their buckskin bags. The feathers that you see are from my youth when I used them to dream out my future. My wish for you is that you may have all my success in your life."

He gave Joseph a funny look. "Um, thanks, but why are you sorry? I mean, you shouldn't be sorry for anything, Grandfather. You're the greatest."

The old man's head dropped to hide the tears welling in his eyes. "A grandfather who cannot serve his grandson should feel the humiliation of all the people."

"S-Serve me? I don't understand."

"Our journey together, young one. I...I cannot continue."

Danny gazed long at Joseph's saddened expression. He wrapped his arms around him, hugging him tightly. They huddled in silence as hot winds rose out of the valley, whipping their hair and stinging their faces.

"I can't leave you," Danny announced suddenly. "I'll just find my answers here."

Joseph managed a smile. "My only grandson...that is what I expected you to say, for you place all others before yourself.

But that would not be the correct path, and you must answer Coyote's call."

"You're more important than Coyote."

"And I will always be with you, Danny. It is your destiny we speak of...your dream, remember?" He patted the boy's hand.

"Besides, we came well prepared for the mountain. I have food, plenty of water, and a warm fire. I will be safe here until you return."

Danny studied him carefully. "Are you sure?" he asked.

"As sure as I am that you will find your true path."

"And I'itoi's cave...I mean, what's wrong with Lion's Ledge? This place is cool. We could have a ceremony around the fire and stuff."

Joseph sighed deeply, his eyes following a distant ridge line. "No, my son, you are Coyote-meeter and he is your life force. Where he leads, you must follow. The ritual to dream your future must be in the place of the Elder Brother—the place of all eternity to the Tohono O'odham—the cave of I'itoi."

"So, it's only me then..." Danny mouthed, staring into the distant valley.

Joseph's eyes glistened. "Yes...for not since the youth of Jonathan Gray Horse has there been such a messenger among us."

"I'll do it, Grandfather...I can do it," he braved. But then his expression changed. "What if I get lost? How do I find I'itoi's cave?"

"Here, help me to stand," Joseph answered. "I have something to show you by the campfire."

When they were settled Joseph selected a chunk of charcoal from the edge of the pit. He turned to study the front of Danny's clothes.

"Take off your tee shirt—I need it for a moment."

"My...what for?"

"Do not worry, I shall return it."

Spreading it on the rock surface, he began to scrape and etch a design on the front. His face was a picture of deep concentration as he worked.

"Grandfather, my shirt," Danny groaned.

"I am sorry, but I did not say in what condition I would return it. Please, this is important, my son."

First, he made a large circle, which he did not close, leaving a small gap in the line. In the gap he drew a human stick figure. Then, around and around inside, he followed the curve of the circle, fashioning a kind of maze; the coils getting ever smaller until they reached the very center. There, he rubbed hard with the charcoal, leaving a heavy black spot.

"I recognize that," said Danny. "It's the man-in-the-maze. We have one on the front of our school. I remember when we did a play about the creation story."

"Yes, there is another on the tribal headquarters building in Sells," Joseph added. "But, only the elders know it has additional meaning—hidden from the human eye."

"Hidden, really?"

He nodded solemnly. "As it has been with our people for all of time...a secret key to the location of the cave of I'itoi."

Danny was puzzled. "It doesn't look like a key to me."

"You must study it more closely, my son. Do you see the figure of I'itoi in the outer circle of the maze? Now, I want you to concentrate on that figure. Do not take your eyes from it."

"Wow, it's moving...slowly, toward the center."

"Ho, and others might say it is going in the opposite direction, leaving the maze. And so, two important stories are kept with the O'odham. One says I'itoi is following life's path with all of its twists and turns until he reaches the center where he pauses to reflect on his life before crossing the final threshold. The other says that he is emerging from Mother Earth into the world with all of us following in like manner."

Danny's brow wrinkled in thought. "So, the gap represents the cave of I'itoi and this line coiling around is a trail leading to the cave."

"That is good," Joseph grinned, "you are quick to see."

"But what I don't get is where the trail starts. Have we been following it?"

A glimmer flashed in Joseph's eye. "Yes, except for the unexpected roundabout when we met those men. But there is still a piece missing." He pointed at their gear. "Fetch me my pack."

Searching inside, Joseph slowly removed a neatly folded antelope skin. The soft hide was deeply yellowed and looked old and fragile. He handled it with great care and reverence. One delicate flap at a time, he opened it and laid it beside the tee shirt.

"Cool, it's like a treasure map," Danny chirped. "And look…'X' marks the spot!"

"It is not a treasure map," Joseph assured, "but rather a journey drawn in pictures. Do you see the twin peaks and Lion's Ledge here?" His bent finger traced over tiny dots and colorful markers. "And next to it, Scorpion's pool?"

"Yeah, now I see, it's Baboquivari. Did you draw this, Grandfather?"

"Yes, a long journey ago when I was not much older than you."

"Then I guess the 'X' is really the cave, right?"

"You are beginning to understand the secret. So, let me ask you what you think of my map?"

Danny scratched his head. "Well, it's very beautiful and all, but if it were lost it wouldn't mean much to whoever found it and tried to read it."

"Exactly," said Joseph, "unless that person also possessed the key." He nodded at the tee shirt.

"Sweet," Danny murmured, his eyes studying the two objects. "The man-in-the-maze…it leads you to the cave."

"Follow these lines on your shirt, my son. They are switchbacks winding to the summit. And watch for landmarks I have drawn on the map, like the place of many oaks near the entrance to the cave. They stand in a group with their arms all touching. When you see them you will know you are near."

Danny held up the design to admire it. "I'll have the key hanging around my neck, sort of." He pulled the tee shirt over his head. "It's an awesome drawing, Grandfather."

"Do you see how quickly things change?" Joseph chided. "Now you are thanking me."

Danny grinned widely. He loved it when Joseph held up a mirror so he could see reflected in it his true self.

25

The rescuers were making excellent time. As the morning sun crept higher in the sky, they crossed the long ridge, passing close to the shade of the palo verde tree where Danny and Joseph had talked strategy the night before. Ahead they saw the walls of a secluded canyon thick with mesquite and scrub oak. Digs Ramirez had just taken his turn on lead when a cry rose from the rear.

"Hold up, guys," Tony puffed. "I'd know this tread anywhere." His eyes followed a faint trace winding uphill from the path. "It's from Danny's hikers. They're the same brand as mine. I don't quite understand this, but for some reason they left the main trail here...and headed up there."

They stood in silent contemplation, staring at the steep embankment. A lone turkey vulture soared in the heavens, disappearing beyond the jagged cliff face above them.

"Holy...that's like suicide," declared Digs. "Oh, uh, sorry, Mr. Rivas, I-I didn't mean that." He avoided Tony's look.

A burst of static from Tom's radio invaded the quiet surroundings. He stepped off the trail to listen to the crackle of a message from Border Patrol.

"We're to proceed with extreme caution," he announced shortly after. "Looks like mules in the canyon ahead. The copter took a bullet, but except for the windshield, no damage."

"That may be why they left the main trail," said Tony. "Old Joseph has the eyes of a hawk."

"It's pretty rugged up there," Tom answered. "Let's hope he has the legs of a mountain goat too. I vote we stay on the main trail and take our chances up ahead. Now that they've been spotted, those illegals ought to be long gone."

"Okay, but if it's all the same to you, Mr. Charro, I'll give up the lead until we get through that canyon," Digs added.

After quick gulps of water, they headed out again with Tom in front. For the rest of the morning their pace was slower and more watchful as they followed the trail through the canyon.

Twice they were forced to halt in the thickets as unidentified sounds echoed off the rock walls. It wasn't the way

Officer Charro usually handled things, but trying to round up illegals wasn't their primary mission. They were climbing the mountain to save lives, preferably without losing their own.

Danny knew about Murphy's Law; that things would go wrong if they could. It was a way of thinking that had worked in the past when he needed a ready excuse for his mistakes. Of course, there had been more recent times when he had basically denied everything and just run away from his problems. Strangely enough though, these shortcut solutions no longer seemed as tempting to him, and that was probably a very good thing as he sat in a cold shiver under an overhanging rock trying to figure his next move.

The rain and wind had come upon him suddenly. It had drenched his clothing and buffeted his body, making it difficult to keep his balance along the narrow trail. After scraping his elbow in a painful fall, he had decided to seek shelter and wait it out.

But now, as he tried to focus his mind on a plan, the chill of loneliness crept over him. He could only think of Joseph left behind, and the misery of the storm pounding Lion's Ledge.

"I never should have gone, Grandfather," he cried into the spray soaking his face. "You were wrong and so was Jonathan Gray Horse...about Coyote, school...about everything."

The fierceness of the wind increased. It blew a gale, drowning out his voice. Thunder boomed and heat lightening snapped overhead.

"Creator, you make noise so you won't have to listen. Do you fear the truth?"

Momentarily, the gusts quieted and the downpour subsided. The sound of the tempest was replaced by the splash and gurgle of water cascading down rock walls. Gullies were carved from the banks as runoff coursed downward. The storm was passing, and all the plants of the high desert glistened and dripped in the fresh breeze.

He peered cautiously out from his retreat at black clouds still rolling and rumbling overhead. An occasional flash broke from within as winds carried the storm northward. The sun appeared briefly and then hid itself again.

"So, you *were* listen..."

Ya ruh, ya ya ya ruh, ra ra ruh, ra ruuuuuuh...

The haunting sound played fatefully in his ears. Even from its distant point near the summit, the lone coyote's call was unmistakable. It echoed across the heights of Baboquivari like a challenge rather than a cry of injury or defense. Danny held his breath waiting for the wail to continue, but it did not return. In its place a restless quiet descended, except for the steady trickle of rainwater.

"That was freaky," he whispered, once back on the trail. "I get mad and the storm stops. Then the coyote...like he understood every word." Casting a wary eye toward the high peak, he made a quick sign of the cross. "Guess I'd better not argue, huh, mountain?"

Onward and upward he hiked, stopping occasionally to study Joseph's map and get his bearings from the design on his shirt. As he picked his way through a stand of ocotillo hugging the hillside, he noticed the path growing fainter and fainter. Finally, it stopped all together at the edge of a deep chasm. Hollowed out by the wind and water of time, the narrow gorge seemed to split the mountain in two, blocking his forward progress.

"Okay, where to?" he breathed.

Advancing cautiously, he peered over the side into the void. From far below, perhaps fifty feet or more, came the roar of a rushing watercourse. Huge boulders loomed out of the fine mist.

"Whoa, long way down."

Backing away from the edge, he took a seat on a rock to study the antelope skin.

"It shows here on the map three flat-topped rocks and a fallen tree," he murmured, "but no drawing of this very dangerous hole in the ground. Grandfather, what should I do?"

He rose to stare up and down the chasm, but nothing seemed to fit with Joseph's careful drawings. The deep crevice ran all the way into the valley below, and curved out of sight in the rock face above him.

I'll bet this tree is a bridge, he thought, *but since this map is almost as old as our family, it probably means the tree rotted years ago and fell in there.*

He shook his head wearily. Pulling the pack off his shoulder, he plunked it on the ground. With his water bottle in hand, he sat on the bag to wash down his disappointment. Just then he spotted something.

"Three flat-topped rocks..."

A short distance back along the trail a massive boulder sat embedded in the hillside. He had passed it without notice on his way through the stand of ocotillos. Now he saw that the top half of the rock was cut off—likely by the powerful hand of the Creator—leaving a perfectly flat surface.

"Let's climb the bank and see what's up there," he whispered.

Arriving on the raised step, he was immediately drawn to a solitary stone positioned, it seemed, in the very center. He lifted the football-sized rock to examine it.

"Wow, there's something carved here."

He rotated it slowly in his hands. "A tarantula? Let's see... one, two, three...yup, eight legs means it's a spider. Cool, I wonder who put it here."

He placed it back with the figure showing. "Anyway, this is where I found you...and this is more than a coincidence."

With his hands shading his eyes, he gazed farther up the bank at the towering cliffs below Baboquivari's eastern summit. A gust of wind grabbed his body forcing him to take a dizzy step backward.

"I knew it!" he blared.

A good distance up the rock-strewn grade was a second boulder; like the first, only smaller. It rested in similar fashion, jutting from the mountainside.

He scrambled eagerly up the sandy wall, spilling an avalanche of volcanic stone behind him. Higher and higher, he slogged, reaching toward the bank for balance. With a final push of his legs, he moved out onto the tabletop.

This time the flat surface was bare with no rock marker to inspect or guide him. He stood in the center with the wind whipping at his face while all around his lofty perch the beauty of the clouds filled him with a new energy. Yet in spite of a careful search of the surrounding landscape, he saw no sign of a third flat rock. He made another turn just to be sure. Nothing; not a single boulder looked like the others.

"I-It can't be," he muttered.

Unfolding the map once more, he grabbed the front of his shirt to stare at the design. His eyes traced feverishly along the maze in the direction of I'itoi's figure.

"First, I took this switchback...right. And then, I made it to here..."

He wasn't sure he heard it the first time, but a sudden shift in the wind brought the faint sound of rushing water. He peered along the hillside to where he thought the noise had originated. Leading away in a thin, twisting line was the vague marking of a footpath. It curved gently out of sight in the direction of the chasm.

Moving quickly, he followed the trace, weaving his way through tangles of cactus and around shapeless slabs of granite. At each turn, the noise grew louder until finally it was the same roar he had heard on the lower trail. Squeezing his body between two giant boulders, he stood once again near the edge of the gorge. A triumphant cry rose from his lips, echoing against the cliffs.

"The tree!"

Wedged tightly between opposite sides of the deep chasm was the giant trunk of an ancient sycamore. Toppled by the fury of a storm, it had tightened its hold on Mother Earth. Gnarled upper branches had penetrated the rock in the far wall, establishing a second root system. Leaves sprouted on saplings rising from underground runners of the old tree.

"Hey, just like the one that saved my life," he grinned.

As he approached, he noticed a flat-topped boulder beneath the tree. A deep crack ran through the center where the fallen sycamore had made impact.

"The rock...it's the third rock," he beamed.

Raising Joseph's weathered map to his lips, he kissed it softly before returning it to the safety of his belt.

26

The auxiliary fuel gauge had hit the half empty mark when Delaney decided to radio the rescue team somewhere on the trail below. For nearly an hour he had traced and retraced the eastern face of Baboquivari without spotting Danny and Joseph.

"Tom, any sign of those illegals in the canyon, over?"

His receiver crackled to life as he piloted the copter along a ridge of densely packed piñon pines. He listened intently while his eyes scoured the ground.

"That's good...I've radioed them in, so they should have a nice reception waiting for them when they come out of the desert. Sorry to say, no sign of our two climbers and my fuel is running low. What's your present location, over?"

Beyond the ridge the terrain opened into a high valley.

Cradled in the middle, a deep blue mountain pond shimmered in the sunlight. Delaney swung his craft in for a closer look.

"Yeah, I know where that is. Okay, good, just keep on the track, boys. I'll be returning to base soon to refuel and I may not be back out here today." He stole another peek at his gauges. "I'm going to make one last run along the saddle toward Lion's Ledge. I doubt they made it that far, but it's worth a quick shot, over."

Hovering above the pond, Delaney carefully tapped on the control stick of the A-Star. His eyes searched the water's edge as he maneuvered the craft in a fixed rotation.

"Right, you've got to push it," he answered. "If I see anything you'll be the first to hear, but it's starting to look like you're their best chance, over and out."

Lifting out of the trees, he turned the copter into the mountain and started his ascent. Above him waited Lion's Ledge and the remote cliffs near Baboquivari's summit. For the first time since leaving Naco Station, he began to wonder if they would ever find Danny and his grandfather alive. As he watched the fuel needle dip dangerously under the strain of full throttle, a scary thought came to mind—would it be necessary for any of them to die trying?

Below him in the shadows, the roar of water over jagged rock was a reminder of the terrible death waiting should he make a single false step. Terror shook Danny's knees and sweat poured down his spine as he inched his way across the immense trunk.

The distance to the far side seemed to increase with each tiny shuffle of his feet. But in spite of the danger he faced, he was still able to focus on a system he'd worked out in his mind: take deep breaths, hold them while sliding each foot forward one length, watch the center of the log—and don't look down.

"This is no time to get cute," he whimpered as the wind began to gust around him.

Extending his arms like a pair of wings, he slowly, painfully, closed in on the opposite bank. At last, he teetered just a few feet from safety. Sucking in one more breath, he bolted across the final distance, coming to a triumphant halt on solid ground. He rested with his hands on his knees trying to calm the shaking.

"Oh, my god," he panted, "I have to come back this way?"

Pulling a single water bottle from under his belt, he took a satisfying drink. He rolled the cold liquid around in his mouth before swallowing. Replacing the cap tightly, he checked the beef jerky he had stashed inside Joseph's map. Slowly unfolding it, he tore off a strip of the meat and chewed it hungrily.

"Sleeping tonight could get uncomfortable," he muttered, glancing back across the chasm, "and I'd better ration this water."

Hanging in open view from the roots of the sycamore was his backpack; tied tightly to keep small animals of the forest from sniffing out the contents. The decision had been made, and once made, could not now be easily undone. Wearing the weighty pack would have been too risky. There would have been no second chance from a fall off the tree.

"I guess it's even more important that I find the cave tonight," he whispered.

Turning quickly, he set out once more on the narrow trail.

Far down the mountain the rescuers pushed on. Stripping off outer shirts and tying bandanas around their heads, they climbed an open ridge under the direct glare of an Arizona sun. Passing through thick clumps of mountain sage, they descended into a ravine, following its twisting course uphill.

Directly above them was the Saddle; a rocky spine arched in the shape of a bow. The trail ran along it like a thin ribbon winding ever upward onto Lion's Ledge.

They moved with determined strides, their eyes focused on the uneven ground. Except for an occasional warning or command, they avoided small talk. Tony was first to break the silence.

"Digs, feel like sharing?" he asked.

"Uh, sure, Mr. Rivas, like what?"

"Well, like you're Danny's best friend...why aren't you with him?"

Digs peeked at him shyly. "That's what Theresa wanted to know. I wanted to be, but he wouldn't let me. I mean, it was his decision and all...said it was just him and Joseph. I could tell from his voice, you know?"

"Yeah, I know...that bond between them."

"I'm sorry, Mr. Rivas, he was acting sort of weird."

"Okay, weird or not, friends usually tell each other everything. Are you sure he didn't say anything else that might help us now?"

"I wish I could remember it all, but I don't think so," said Digs. "He did mention the cave, but we know about that already."

"Yes, I'm sure that's his goal."

"And among us O'odham," broke in Tom, "it is also known that the trail is difficult to follow with many switchbacks and dead ends. Add to this an eighty year-old man slowing them down..."

"Please, don't remind me,'Tony grumbled.

"Listen Tone, that's exactly my point. We're bound to catch up to them soon."

"I sure hope so. The more this drags on, the more worried I get. And I don't even want to think about Cecilia."

"Come on, Mr. Rivas," Digs braved, "he's right, we'll be spotting them soon...even before we get to that Lion's place."

The wind blew at their backs as they climbed the side of a huge boulder and started up the narrow spine of the Saddle.

Delaney slowed his air speed on the approach to Lion's Ledge. As his eyes traced along the shelf, he marveled at the force of nature to heave the massive strata out from the mountain. Carefully, he maneuvered the craft closer, mindful of strong wind currents that could pull him into the rocks. The propellers of the A-Star 350 fought the push of warm air being thrust back from the walls.

Whuuump, whuuump, whuuump, whuuump, whuuump.

He pulled back from the cliff while his eyes searched the ledge for any sign of movement. Just then he spotted a wisp of smoke from a tiny campfire and the figure of someone huddled next to it. Dangerous updrafts buffeted the craft as he drifted in for a closer look.

"Tom, it's Delaney, over."

He waited anxiously for his long-time friend on the reservation police to respond.

"I'm up on Lion's Ledge...a-and I think I've got the old man."

The draft from the propellers pounded the ledge, sending dust and soot swirling above the fire pit.

"I don't see Danny, but...Joseph...he's not moving...he's not moving."

Part Four

Baboquivari

27

Wooooooooooosssh, woooooooooooosssh, wooooooooooosssh.

Wind poured through a narrow opening in the rock above Danny's head. The sound reminded him of Santa Ana night breezes that often awakened him in his room. Blowing in through the open window, they would rattle the pane and flutter the curtains. Feeling the chill, he'd pull the sheet up tight to his chin, uncovering his toes to the cool air. Oddly enough, he liked the feel of air-conditioned feet. He wished he was home right now—under the covers, safe and secure.

Resting his back against the ledge, he pulled the map from his shirt. He'd had little need of it over the last mile or so. Although faint in places, the path had been easier to follow without the mysterious switchbacks below the chasm, but now he stood once again at a seemingly unsolvable dead end. He stared at the wall in front of him, listening to wind rush through a hole near the top.

"This is strange," he mused, tapping the antelope skin with his finger. "Looks like a dust devil or a whirlwind. And what's this dotted line running through the middle?"

He studied the maze on his shirt again to make sure he was in the right location. Slowly and carefully his eyes followed the zigzag in the design.

153

"Yeah, I'm at the picture of the whirlwind, all right. So, on the rest of the map a dotted line represents a trail. That means..."

The swirling air current nearly tore the map from his grasp. He cursed softly, turning his back to the wind.

"...the correct path...I get it!" he yelped. "I'm *in* the whirlwind, which means the trail leads through there." He pointed up at the small hollow in the rock. "Right, I just climb this wall like a lizard and crawl through a hole barely bigger than...Pepito, the Chihuahua."

He sat with a broken look, staring at the little drawing on the skin. Up to this point, he'd found answers to Joseph's challenges, but this one seemed impossible.

"Grandfather, you're kidding. What am I to do, fly?"

With his body worn from the climb, he laid his head on the map and closed his eyes to rest. Maybe a clear mind could come up with a plan, he thought, as he drifted to sleep.

"I need a rope or something," he yawned, stretching the muscles in his legs after his half-hour nap. "I'll never know if that opening is big enough unless I can reach it."

He had jumped awake with his eyes on the sun as it dropped lower in the western sky. Thankfully, he'd only slept for a short time.

"Yes, or something," he repeated, walking slowly back along the trail. "I can climb a rock...Hmm, a big one is too heavy, but two smaller ones stacked against the wall, maybe. That would make me a tall person."

He remembered how he and Joseph had used an ocotillo shaft to pull themselves up that lower wall. But he realized as he scanned the sparse vegetation that the plant didn't grow at such a high altitude. He paced back and forth, his mind digging for a solution.

Staring at a pair of piñon pines hugging the mountainside, he suddenly hit upon an idea. Thick clusters of green cones hanging from the branches meant the trees were at the peak of annual growth. He knew from Joseph's lessons that the tree's thick, gooey sap was also running. Amber colored masses of sticky liquid oozed down the trunks. If he could find one or two gobs of the sweet smelling resin, he might be able to put them to good use.

"Maybe I can be a lizard after all," he chirped.

Circling the tree heaviest with cones, he made a quick inspection of the trunk. Vertical streaks of sap ran to the base, collecting there in large clumps. Moving beneath the branches, he used a stick to scrape off the yellowish liquid.

Lifting the mass gingerly, he passed it from hand to hand. The lump of pitch stuck to his fingers like glue, spreading quickly onto his wrists. He smeared his arms up to his elbows, rubbing some on the front of his shirt and jeans and the toes of his hiking boots. The piney substance felt stiff and uncomfortable plastered to his clothing, but it would be worth it if his idea worked.

Returning to the place of the whirlwind, he slid a watermelon-sized rock up against the barrier. Standing atop it, he reached high up the surface with his arms, firmly pressing his body to the stone. Slowly, carefully, he lifted his feet, digging his toes into the wall. There, he hung motionless like a spider clinging to its web.

"Uuhhh, okay, easy does it," he grunted as he inched up the steep incline.

After tense moments and a couple of slips, he finally was able to crawl within arms length of the opening in the rock. He stared intently at the hole trying to decide if there was enough room for his body to fit through.

"Hmm, it seems a little bigger up close than it did from below."

Gathering his energy, he made a lunge for the opening. His arm caught the bottom edge leaving his body dangling in space. Desperately, he struggled to gain a toehold on the rock. Finally catching the sole of one boot, he grabbed the edge with his other arm. Gradually, he hoisted himself up, poking his head through the narrow gap.

"This is it," he breathed, his eyes picking up the trail again as it snaked its way up the rocky embankment beyond. "Grandfather, how in the world did you get past this hole?"

Squirming and twisting his body, he squeezed through the tight space. He sat shaking his head at the opening. "There must have been a rope or ladder here once, is all I can say."

Safely back on the trail, he pulled out the map for another look. Although the front of his tee shirt was now a gummy mess, the outer rings of the maze were still visible.

"Cool, I'm near the top," he beamed, "so I don't need the maze. After the whirlwind, the last drawing is the place of many oaks. Joseph said the cave is nearby."

With the sun rapidly descending, the eastern face of Baboquivari now lay in shadows. He gazed along the cliff where pockets of darkness hid desert dwellers, lurking in the hollows and crevices of the rocks. Once the black of night was upon him, the trail would be unsafe. One wrong step might be his last. He set off at a trot, knowing he must reach the shelter of the cave quickly.

"We've got him from here, Burt," Tom answered. "I'd say half an hour and we'll be on the ledge." A noisy raven rode the thermals overhead. "You've done all that you can for now, over and out."

Tony stared anxiously at his friend. "What's the report?"

"Well, it d-doesn't look good for Joseph," he announced. "Burt says he isn't moving. Come on, we need to pick up the pace."

"What about Danny?"

"No sign of him on the ledge, but Burt can't wait...he's got to return to base for fuel."

"Yeah, okay, so l-like you said, let's go." Tony bolted across the top of a boulder.

"Easy, my friend, we *are* in the mountains," he warned. "Let's just maintain a steady pace. I mean, no sense in us getting hurt."

"But Danny..."

"I'm sure he's all right, Mr. Rivas," Digs inserted. "Joseph has taught him a lot about survival, you know."

"Yes, but that's survival in the desert," he breathed, "this is Baboquivari."

Winding through thick brush and over tracts of loose rock, they climbed the ridge with renewed urgency.

28

Danny could see the entrance to I'itoi's cave. He was sure of it, even though he'd never climbed Baboquivari before. It lay partially hidden in a tiny glen not more than a few hundred feet from the summit. The trail wound through waist-high grass into a grove of tough and wind-battered oaks. It had the feel of an honored place; a secluded sanctuary on the edge of nature's tempest, dangerously close to the fury of the storm, yet when entered, strangely quiet and peaceful.

With his eyes fixed on the dark opening in the cliff wall, he made his way among the trees, slowing his pace as he approached. Now he saw signs of its sacredness; flat rocks had been stacked to form cairns on either side of the entrance while a number of small artifacts—carved stone figures, tiny hand-woven baskets containing feathers and bits of turquoise, and a finely crafted child's olla—had been perfectly positioned to guard the threshold. A sage bundle used by visitors to purify their movements had been wedged in a crack in the wall. Peering into the shadows, he noticed more objects just inside; family photos and prayer sticks scattered about.

He dropped to his knees at the place where Elder Brother emerged from Mother Earth to join Earthmaker and Buzzard. Reaching into his shirt and pockets, he searched for an offering; a gift to leave at this most holy of shrines. Unfolding Joseph's antelope skin map, he carefully laid it among the pictures on the sandy floor of the cave.

"I'm here, Grandfather...I made it," he announced, his voice echoing out of the narrow cavern. "Like you taught me...the place where we came into the world after the great flood."

He stared into the black recesses of the cave, listening for Joseph's answer amidst a commotion of whistling wind. He tried forming; shaping the rushing, rustling sounds into something recognizable, but even a boy's most vivid imagination couldn't conjure up words. With a lonely sigh, he sat cross-legged in a spot where he could watch the trail, and waited.

"It's bad enough that I talk to myself all the time," he mumbled, "but now I'm expecting someone to talk back. Must be I'm oxygen deprived."

He poked with a twig in the soft sand. "Who am I kidding? I came all this way for basically nothing. There aren't any answers here...not from Joseph <u>or</u> Coyote."

He watched dejectedly as the sun's golden glow slowly faded beyond the mountaintop. Nothing in the world, it seemed, was right about the decision to leave his grandfather and climb to the top of a mountain looking for answers to life's questions. Answers he could just as easily find at home. That is, nothing except the words of Joseph, himself.

"I'm here because you wanted me to go on, Grandfather. I mean, you're the one who called me the coyote-meeter and everything. And you're always right. So, what do I do now?"

The wind blew harder across the tops of the trees, making their gnarled branches rattle. He glanced nervously about as murmuring sounds broke from the grass thickets and a whisper of voices was heard among the scrub oaks. A fine dust swirled about the entrance to the cave, forcing him to shield his eyes.

"Who's there?" he called.

But only the wind answered him, gusting and whistling among the boulders. He listened to the sounds, hugging his knees close to his body.

"What am I, loony? There's no one else here."

Just then, a faint humming began in the back of the trees, steadily growing to the sound of a swarm. He stared into the gathering twilight, trying to spot movement or see shapes in the shadows, but nothing stirred along the trail through the grass.

Suddenly the wind died, while all through the glen the awful buzzing grew more powerful. It reverberated in his ears, forcing him to slap his hands against them. His teeth chattered uncontrollably.

"I asked who was there," he cried out.

The sound of bees continued as shadows lengthened on the walls around the cave. He rose carefully and moved away from the entrance, standing with his back against the stone.

"Okay, this is crazy. I'm not going to hide here like a wimp."

Gathering his wits, he stepped forward, inching his way along the path through the tall grass. The twisted shapes of black oaks closed around him as he moved deeper into the glen. But he had made his move and there was no turning back. And all the while, that terrible sound grew louder and louder.

They climbed the last slide of crumbled rock and walked out onto the level surface of Lion's Ledge. Tony led the exhausted hikers along the narrow rift that skirted the east face of the mountain. Tom and Digs followed closely, hugging the cliff wall as far back from the edge as possible.

It had been a forced march to reach Joseph and the effort had taken its toll. Their clothes were soaked with perspiration and sweat dripped from the ends of their noses. Their shoulders were hunched and they stubbed an occasional toe as they walked. Yet in spite of their bedraggled look, they kept a hopeful eye on the trail ahead. Digs was first to spot the huddled figure beside the campfire.

"Mr. Rivas, he's there...look!"

They scrambled forward, stumbling recklessly as they went. Dropping their backpacks to the ground, they quickly formed a circle around Joseph.

Tony grasped the old man's shoulders, staring keenly at his face. Joseph slumped in his arms, his eyelids fluttering wildly. "Hay-nah-waaah..." he mumbled.

"Joseph," Tony cried, "you're alive! Jiosh i wehmtaDag ahni, God help us, you're alive."

The elder blinked repeatedly, awakening from his trance. He pushed Tony back with a start. "A-And why shouldn't I be?" he breathed suddenly. "Our mission is not over and I must concentrate."

They were speechless, gazing wide-eyed at Joseph's determined expression. Finally Tom, and then Digs, managed to pull their eyes away, but Tony remained a captive.

"C-Concentrate?" he spluttered.

"Yes, Danny has arrived at the place of our birth and is with the spirits now. It is important that I remain close to guide him."

"Joseph, you can't be…"

"Please, my son," he insisted, "Danny faces a great challenge and I must continue my meditation. I will need some water now. When next I open my eyes it will be over…and then I will eat."

"But we need to go after him," Tony pleaded.

"We should not interfere, for he is safe at the cave of I'itoi." Joseph motioned with a weak hand. "All of you…keep me company. Water…please, some water."

Tony retrieved his pack, handing Joseph a bottle. He drank deeply before settling back into position. With his eyes tightly closed, he bowed his head and took several deep, relaxing breaths. Ever so slowly, his shoulders straightened and he raised an arm toward the sky.

"Kaidam, ahni ne'ichud ahpi," he chanted, "loudly, I sing for you, dear Grandson."

Tom rose from the circle, motioning quietly to Tony. They moved out of earshot to discuss their next move.

"Tony, I understand that Joseph is a makai…uh, into spiritual healing and all, but can we really be sure he's right about Danny?"

"I don't know," he muttered. "They really click, but I don't think anyone should be hiking up there alone."

"So, do we go along with him or not?"

Tony winced. "Damn, I hate this, but it's getting dark and we can't climb until morning. We're out of choices, I'm afraid."

"I'll radio the copter about tomorrow then," Tom answered. He gently patted Tony's shoulder. "You wanna' tell Digs? In the meantime, we're just going to have to grin and bear it."

"Yeah," Tony sighed, "wish I could grin. I haven't been able to for a long time though."

29

Deafening now was the swarming sound as Danny followed the path deeper into the trees. From out of the grass, flying insects began to circle his head and shoulders, swooping and darting, hitting his face and bouncing away. Hornets and deer flies, yellow jackets and wasps buzzed about his eyes and ears; some trying to land while others simply hovered close to his body.

He tried swatting and wiping them away, but his efforts were fruitless as the winged invaders continued to swarm over him. Many clung desperately to his form as he walked, refusing to let go. Soon his hands and arms were covered with a thick layer of crawling, wriggling insects. He cast a frightened eye toward the deepening shadows of the glen as more and more attackers rose from the thickets.

It was then he realized that none of his tormentors were stinging or biting him. No matter how hard he cuffed and swiped they never grew angry. He was being harassed for sure; all about his face and neck, but not injured.

"This is a sign...a warning. I'm too close," he breathed. "God, w-what should I do?"

His body was suddenly gripped by a terror greater than any he had ever known. Fear and uncertainty had quickly penetrated the deepest parts of his being. His entire torso shook and his heart pounded uncontrollably.

Joseph's foretelling of a spirit world beyond the night was as real to him now as were these guardians of sacred ground; swarming about his arms and crawling inside his shirt. He froze in his tracks at a new sound; close by, rising to mix with the multitude.

Ya ya ya ruuuh, ya ruuuuuuuuuh.

The animal cry had come from just ahead in the grass. Very slowly, he began to back down the trail.

"Coyote, is it you?" he voiced.

Two yellow eyes appeared on the path in front of him. They remained stationary for a time, but as he continued his backward steps the eyes carefully followed—back through the trees and out of the grass, always keeping a safe distance.

As he reached the mouth of I'itoi's shrine the swarm of insects scattered, disappearing into the dark. The awful sound in the trees quickly died away, replaced by an eerie quiet, while directly in front of him the watching eyes of Coyote waited.

He knelt inside the opening, never allowing the mysterious twin spots to leave his sight. So far, the wild dog's form had not been revealed, in spite of Danny's efforts to draw him closer. And when several more minutes passed without sound or movement from the animal, his patience began to run thin.

"I know you...from the wash and at Scorpion's pool."

No sooner had he spoken the words than the coyote stepped out in the open. Its body was immense; just as Danny remembered, and still covered with a dark brown coat. Its legs were long and powerful with a large head like a wolf. It hesitated a few feet away, watching him closely, without the growling and snarling in the wash.

Danny took a deep breath and continued. "And you know me too, isn't that right?"

The coyote licked its chops and whined nervously. Dropping its nose to the sand, it sniffed the track where Danny had walked.

"I would never have thought of coming here, but..."

The coyote's ears perked. It was watching him again with those wild eyes—the ones that didn't seem so wild all of a sudden.

"What I mean is, I'm sorry I just showed up without asking, but Grandfather kind of insisted."

The coyote's upper lip curled, revealing a long, sharp fang.

"Okay, okay, it was my idea too."

Maybe it was a better idea, he thought, to follow what was in his heart. His eyes and his voice softened.

"Anyway, if you really know me then you know about Joseph, and my mom and dad, and my sister, Sophie, and Mr. Jensen, who wants me to go to..."

Ya ya ya ruuuuuuh.

The coyote raised its head into the night air.

"I d-didn't mean..."

Suddenly turning its back, the dog trotted down the path out of sight. A few moments later, it returned to sit at the edge of the clearing. There, it waited once again, gently testing the breeze with its nose.

A long minute passed before it rose for a second time and disappeared into the blackness, only to reappear a bit farther down the trail. It quickly selected a place and settled down, watching him carefully.

"You want me to follow..."

He stood by the entrance to the cave. "But, don't you realize? I can't, it's too dark."

At a time like this, he sure wished Joseph was around. He studied the figure of the coyote waiting in the grass.

"Grandfather, what is he trying to say?"

Above him in the Arizona sky, stars hung in a giant canopy. They sent glitters and sparkles down from light years away to the tiny glen. Danny focused on one particular gem in the area where Dr. Richards had helped him identify Virgo. It seemed to vanish and then reappear—just as Coyote had.

And then it hit him like a monsoon bolt of lightning.

"I understand now," he breathed. "Mom...Dad...I understand!"

Joseph's head jerked and his eyes grew wide. He began to rock back and forth while the first notes of a chant-like song rose from his lips.

"Yaa, yaa, ishta-caa, neseema-caa, yaca-daa..."

From beneath his robe came a gourd rattle, which he gently tapped against his leg. The rapping and shaking gradually increased and his singing continued in a strange chatter.

Digs watched him curiously. "He's not making any sense," he whispered in Tom's ear.

"Hmm, well, maybe not to us, but that's intentional."

"Intentional? I don't get it."

Tom motioned him away from the pit. "I've heard makai's in ceremony and their songs are special...too precious for the rest of us to learn."

"You mean they make up words?"

"Not exactly," he replied, "but they do try to mask their voice to keep us from understanding."

"Cool, so what do you *think* he's saying?"

"Like I said, I don't know, but it's about Danny, no doubt."

The three sat in respectful silence for over an hour as Joseph continued his ritual. After each song he paused, waving an arm slowly above his head. Finally it ended, almost as quickly as it began. The last echoes of the weird singing faded against the walls of distant canyons.

Joseph straightened, flexing his neck and shoulders. He smiled confidently at the hikers.

"Help me to my feet," he ordered. "My legs are stiff and I must walk a while."

"So, what's up?" asked Tony, grasping Joseph under the arm and lifting him easily. "Uh, h-how's Danny? Have you seen him?"

"Our son is safe for now. He will sleep long tonight in the cave of I'itoi."

"How do you know this?"

Joseph smiled at him in silence. Finally, he turned and walked slowly across the open expanse of the ledge. When he reached the far rim he stood staring into the night.

"Danny and I are one," he began. "One with each other and with the souls of our people. These things are not quickly revealed or easily understood, but I have come to know that he is Coyote-meeter, and possesses a gift." He faced them and started back. "This gift...he could not refuse it or ignore the responsibility it brought him. But he no longer stands in the shadows, angry and afraid, for he has traveled I-itoi's maze and grown stronger and wiser."

"He told me at school he needed to do this alone," said Digs.

Joseph approached, placing a hand on his shoulder. "This is why I could not go with him to the cave, my son. But your friend will return to be with you." He turned his attention to Tony. "And what about you, have you also traveled I-itoi's maze?"

Tony nodded quietly. "I have changed directions. Cecilia and Sophie know...and Danny will soon...that I now follow the good, red road."

Tom Charro scratched his neck, studying his friend shyly.

"Good, because he is waiting on that road, and you cannot make things better between you unless you are willing to walk it with him."

"Yup, you're right." He smiled weakly, shaking the old man's hand. "Darn it, Joe, if you aren't always right. In the morning we should start up after him, don't you think?"

"In the morning we will wait," Joseph answered, "for Danny to find us here. It is the right way and do not fear." Before retiring to the fire pit, he thankfully gripped the hand of each rescuer. "And now I will eat."

30

Danny lifted his head from the sand and peered through early morning sunlight streaming into the cave. Gently flexing his leg muscles, he rolled onto one side to gain a better view of the trail. Even though he had slept soundly through the night, a single thought still remained in his mind—the coyote.

And there, in the exact spot where he had last seen it, the wild dog waited. It watched him as before; motionless, with its eyes trained on the cave mouth. A breeze through the oaks ruffled the black fur on its back and around its neck. Was it possible Coyote hadn't moved all night?

Just then, it rose to its feet, edging forward on the path. It tested the air in Danny's direction, and suddenly, without warning, spun about and vanished in the tall grass.

"Ayee," Danny cried, "will I ever see you again?"

He listened to the wind and watched the rays of the sun climb above the distant peaks. A brilliant new day had dawned in the desert, and Danny knew it to be special for one very important reason. Before it ended, he would be reunited with Joseph and his family, ready to share news of his adventure. He'd tell them about Coyote and facing the spirits of his people, about his bravery and finding his true path in life—a great vision that would guide him always.

The descent to Lion's Ledge would be difficult; filled with challenge and danger, but he knew failure was not an option. If he did not return, the knowledge and experience he had gained would be lost to those he loved the most, and to all the Tohono O'odham people whose ancestors had visited him during his hour of struggle.

It was time to leave the cave of I-itoi, but first he must thank the Creator for his new knowledge and perform a ritual to protect his physical and spiritual body. Retrieving a wooden match from deep in his pocket, he plucked loose the bundle of sage wedged in the cave wall. The pale green herb still smelled fresh like the desert after a rain. Striking the match on a rock, he lit the bundle, turning it carefully to allow the embers to spread. Soon the sweet smoke was drifting around his head, forming a cloud in the tight interior of the cave.

With one hand, he pulled the smoke into his face, allowing it to bathe his features. He continued until the heat of the tiny flame reached his fingertip. Dropping the last burning bit into the sand, he snuffed out the glow with his foot.

Gazing once more about the floor of the cave, he studied the gifts brought to pay homage to Elder Brother. Each object, in its own way, emitted the love expressed by its giver. He rubbed the soft surface of Joseph's antelope map, not certain he would ever see it again. When he had finished his quiet vigil, and with renewed purpose, he rose quickly and turned toward the light.

Passing the spot where he had last seen Coyote, he hesitated, resisting the temptation to look back. His mission was not complete and he knew Joseph was waiting. Making his way among the rock slabs and boulders, he started his climb down the mountain.

Tony had lost his patience and the frustration was about to boil over.

"Joseph, we're aware of your place in the tribe, but this isn't about you now, it's about Danny."

"As I have said, he is safe."

"Listen, I'm not going to argue with you about the power of faith. I mean, let's face it, I'm probably the last person on the reservation to go to for advice about anything spiritual."

Joseph's eyes remained steady. "It is true that I cannot stop you from going after him, but I would ask you to stand in the place of another for a moment."

"You mean think like I'm Danny," he answered.

"No, I mean use your heart and mind to consider one among us who is the oldest, yet the youngest, weakest, yet the strongest, poorest, yet the richest."

"I don't…"

"He is Jonathan Luhya Gray Horse, Elder of the Tohono O'odham, and known by our people as Coyote-meeter."

"Yes, of course, I know of him, but…"

"Do you know he speaks of our boy in the same way? Danny is the coyote-meeter." Joseph's crooked hand grasped Tony by the arm. "He is only the second in many generations of our people, my son."

Tony stood by numbly, unable to move or speak. Nothing sounded on the ledge but the faint call of chickadees. Digs was first to break the silence.

"Mr. Estes, will Danny still be like normal when he returns?"

A broad smile cracked Joseph's face. "It is because you are friends and you know each other well that your question is so funny."

"I mean, will he act like everything's cool?"

"Yes," he winked, "he will not act cold, but he will act cool."

"Okay, I get it…I guess."

"So, I will ask you all to be patient for a short time longer to allow Danny to finish what he has started. His journey has been difficult, but in order for it to have true meaning in his life, he must walk it alone. Otherwise, it will have been in vain."

"Okay," another hour or so," Tony declared, "but after that I'm going to have to disappoint you."

Joseph nodded. "It will not be necessary for an hour…"

From a rock-strewn ravine above Lion's Ledge came the sound of a branch snapping underfoot.

"Danny?"

Tony scampered to the back of the ledge and into the evergreen thickets. Cracking and rustling noises followed his path of movement up the mountainside. And then all was suddenly quiet.

Anxious moments passed before sounds from the far end of the ledge attracted their attention. Around an outcropping of rock, two figures were seen approaching.

"Very cool," beamed Digs, running to meet them.

Behind Tom Charro's sturdy figure waited a frail old man with a gleam of excitement in his eyes. Joseph clasped his hands together in eager anticipation.

31

Digs' face was aglow as he raced to Danny's side. They slapped and poked each other playfully.

"Muchacho, was I worried about you or what?" he cried.

"Hey, Man, good to..." Danny's look suddenly soured. "Um, yeah, well, weren't you supposed to keep all this a secret?"

Digs' eyes widened. "W-Well, what was I supposed to do? I had to tell Theresa. She was worried big time. A-And, boy... when a girl wants to put on the pressure, well...s-she just kept bugging me. But the thing is, she's real smart, and so when I told her, she freaked. I-I didn't call your parents, she did."

"Likely story," Danny grumbled with just a hint of a smile.

"Listen, he's right," said Tony. "And I'd say you're lucky to have him for a friend. Would you climb a mountain to save his life?"

"Yup, you bet I would..."

"So, there you go," he shot back. "Now, what I'm interested in hearing is..."

"Sorry, Dad, in just a minute, okay?"

Spotting the figure of Joseph, he broke loose and was soon hugging him tightly.

"My heart is full of gladness, my son," he chuckled.

"You were right, Grandfather. You were right the whole time."

Tony broke in from behind. "Yes, and we both know that now," he said, nodding at the old man.

Joseph responded, "I believe Danny has much to share, but maybe food and water should come first."

"Here, have some of mine," said Digs, passing his canteen.

Danny drank deeply, pouring some over his head and shoulders. "Thanks, but I'm not very hungry, and yeah I do have a lot to say...to you, Grandfather...and to you too, Dad. It's just that I was hoping I could tell you and Mom at the same time."

"That's okay, son," assured Tony, "we'll tell her together."

"That would be great, Dad," he smiled, "and wow...you guys climbed all this way for us?"

"Uh, yeah, that's a fact," he replied, wiping sweat from his brow. "Now, here's a question worth asking. Did you two really think you could pull this off without getting hurt?"

"But we did just fine, didn't we, Grandfather?"

"There's no way we could have known that," Tony responded, "and what about Tom taking time off regular duty and the helicopter from Border Patrol?"

"Border Patrol? Whoa," breathed Danny.

"It turned out all right though," Tom admitted, "plus, we picked up some smugglers along the way."

"Hey, we saw those men. They looked mean and one guy had a gun."

Tony nodded soberly. "So, you see what kind of a fix you nearly got into?"

"Sorry, Dad, but we were never in trouble," he replied, smiling at Joseph, "we were too smart for them."

"Well, all I can say is your friend, Theresa, was very convincing about the danger you were in."

"And we're not off the mountain yet," added Tom.

"Right, so maybe you're ready to admit that we might just come in handy the rest of the way."

Danny lowered his head shyly. "I am glad you came, really. And I'm sorry for the trouble I caused."

Joseph cleared his throat. "Our journey together was honorable, but I accept blame from those who do not approve," he said, eyeing Danny proudly. When no one answered, he continued. "Then all is good and we should return to the campfire. We must eat to gain strength and there is much for us to learn. Danny, take Digs to find wood for our cooking."

"We shouldn't wait long to start back," Tom advised.

"It is important that we listen to our young brother," said Joseph. "We can still reach Pitoikam by nightfall."

Within minutes, a fresh fire was burning in the pit. The group rested against their packs, watching the yellow flames flicker. Shafts of sunlight broke through the clouds onto the ledge, giving the scene added radiance. With strips of beef jerky roasting on sharpened sticks and Cecilia's foil-wrapped fry bread warming in the coals, all eyes turned toward Danny.

"Coyote was there, Grandfather," he began, "but the fire and wildness was gone from his eyes."

"Tell us of your adventure, my son."

"Well, it was about the hardest thing I've ever done, and I would have gotten lost without the map and the maze."

"The maze?" Tony asked. "What about it?"

"Some things are better left from the story," Joseph winked.

"Um, and the three flat-topped rocks were tricky," Danny continued, "I almost missed the last one."

The old man shifted his weight uncomfortably. "Please, start with the cave of I'itoi and your meeting with Coyote."

"When I got to the cave there was this awful buzzing in the trees and these bees swarmed all over me, but they didn't sting. It was very weird."

"The spirits of our people," whispered Joseph.

"Anyway, that's when I heard Coyote and saw him standing on the path. Only, this time he was calm, not growling like before. He kept leaving and coming back. Finally, he just waited...never took his eyes off me. But it wasn't until after dark that I really understood."

"I'm kind of lost, I'm afraid," Tony murmured.

Danny paused to collect his thoughts. "This may not...make sense to you, but the stars did the same thing. They disappeared and then reappeared. So it was a sign...a sign to follow. Coyote wanted me to follow him back down the mountain...to Grandfather...to you, Dad, and Mom and Sophie...to my home and friends where I belong. Don't you see?" His eyes filled with tears. "I don't want to leave San Xavier."

Dapples of shadow and sunlight played upon the faces of the listeners, hiding their expressions. Tony leaned forward quickly.

"Leave San Xavier...where did that idea come from?"

"I was getting ready to tell you," Danny croaked. "T-That is, Grandfather and I were about to. But we needed answers first."

"Please, go on,"Tony nodded,"and don't leave out any details."

"You see, Mr. Jensen at school says I'm good at science... really good," he sniffed. "S-So he wants me to go to a special academy in Colorado. He said there are scholarships and stuff. Well, at first I didn't want to, and then I did..."

"Danny came to me for help with this," said Joseph, "for he knows that I would not deny him. But the road ahead was hidden from view and we needed to walk it together, that is all."

"And now I know what I will tell Mr. Jensen. I will tell him I want to stay here at San Xavier School. I must follow my true calling and try to make my life better...here on the reservation." He wiped the tears from his eyes. "I think I will go to college some day. Don't you think so too, Dad? Maybe even to the University of Arizona."

"If you set your mind to it,"Tony answered quietly.

"And Mr. Jensen will still be around to help," Danny added.

"The decision has been difficult, but it has been your own," said Joseph. "This is what it means to be a leader among the O'odham and you will always stand strong and proud among your people...wherever you journey, my son."

Danny cast a soulful eye at Tony. "Grandfather's birthday at Peña Blanca Lake...That's how I want us to be from now on. Can we, Dad?"

He hugged Tony, hiding his face against his chest. He remembered the peppery smell of the lotion his father shaved with—it had been so long. He could feel the powerful muscles in his arms and he longed to be like him; strong and unafraid. And he just knew Tony wouldn't drink anymore, wouldn't use that language with Cecilia, wouldn't look at him and Sophie with those angry eyes. He would stay home and love them all the same. Danny was sure of it, just as sure as the sun passing high over Baboquivari and the hoot of a pygmy owl atop a mesquite tree.

Tony held Danny's face in his big hands. "I have a lot of apologies to make to you, and I'm starting now. But I want you to know something else...I love you more than words can say, and I'm proud of you for everything that you are."

Tears streamed down Danny's cheeks as he gazed into his father's eyes. He could see truth in them—truth to the depths of Tony's soul. Just then he felt the arms of another. It was Joseph, hugging them from behind.

"Grandfather," he asked, "can we go to Sheep's Head Rock next weekend?"

Tony looked down with a grin. "That's where you were supposed to be...this weekend."

"I will speak to the White Shadow about his problem with directions," laughed Joseph.

When they had eaten, they buried the fire pit and started the descent from Lion's Ledge. Atop a ridge, Danny turned with Joseph for a last look at the peak of the mountain.

"Your map, Grandfather, I left it in the cave."

"I cannot think of a better gift," Joseph whispered with a smile.

Additional Books Recommended for Students

Open Books Press

Moochi's Mariachis
by Mary Ann Hutchison
(Fourth to Ninth grade)

Turtle's Dream
by Delphina Nova
(Picture book with Navaho illustrations and translation)

Pen & Publish

Maggie Ray;
World War II Air Force Pilot
by Marsha J. Wright
(Fourth grade to Adult)

The Write Time: 366 Exercises to
Fulfill Your Daily Writing Life
by Robert Yehling
(Teen to Adult)

Transformation Media Books

Moneylicious:
A Financial Clue for Generation Y
by Ornella Grosz
(Teen to Adult)

About the Author

Robert L. Hunton is the author of novels of mystery and adventure for young readers, including the *Borderlands Trilogy—Gift of the Desert Dog* (2010), *Secrets of the Medicine Pouch: Adventure in the Borderlands* (2011), and *Coyote-meeter's Abyss: Adventure in the Borderlands* (2012).

Hunton's career as a middle school teacher in the Colchester, Vermont School District spanned thirty-two years, during which time he taught 7th and 8th grade language arts/social studies lessons on topics as diverse as cartoon storyboards, Plains Indian winter counts, and medieval castle construction, in places extending beyond the classroom—under a cantilevered rock on a mountainside, in the sanctuary of old barns and covered bridges, or in the woods surrounding Fort Ticonderoga on Lake Champlain, where he walked with his students in the footsteps of Montcalm, Washington, and Ethan Allen.

He has delivered graduation addresses, conducted workshops on curriculum and website development, hammered nails with a president, coached boy's and girl's basketball, and led cub scouts in Blue and Gold banquet songs. He is an active member of the League of Vermont Writers, the Society of Children's Book Writers and Illustrators, and the Society of Southwestern Authors, currently serving as president.

In the winter of 2007, while completing research for *Gift of the Desert Dog*, Hunton appeared with his manuscript before the Tohono O'odham tribal council in Sells, Arizona. He had requested the meeting to ask elders for permission to use O'odham symbols in his book. While he waited nervously before them, they deliberated on his request, conversing in tongue before finally addressing him in English. They would give him the permission he sought! They also thanked him for his respectful consideration of their traditions and customs; a gesture they had rarely experienced from outsiders. The elders were more interested in his use of 'Coyote' in the novel. They related the importance of the creation story among the O'odham, and Coyote's pivotal role. Hunton listened to council suggestions and concerns, returning to the *Gift* manuscript to craft a scene in which Joseph teaches the creation story to Danny.

The author now lives with wife, Julie, near Tucson, Arizona.

Visit Hunton at www.robertlhunton.com and post a comment at www.desertdogblog.blogspot.com.

Contact the author for bookings and signings at National Writers Literary Agency, c/o Andrew Whelchel, at 720-851-1950 or at a.whelchel@globaltalentreps.com.

Source Materials for Teachers

A Natural History of the Sonoran Desert, Steven J. Phillips & Patricia Wentworth Comus, Arizona-Sonora Desert Museum Press, Univ. of California Press.

Animal Energies, Gary Buffalo Horn Man, Dancing Otter Publishing.

Answered Prayers: Miracles and Milagros Along the Border, Eileen Oktavec, Bernard Fontana, Univ. Arizona Press.

Beliefs and Holy Places: A Spiritual Geography of the Pimeria Alta, James S. Griffith, Univ. Arizona Press.

Cultures of Habitat: On Nature, Culture, and Story, Gary Paul Nabhan, Counterpoint.

Enduring Seeds: Native American Agriculture and Wild Plant Conservation, Gary Paul Nabhan, North Point Press.

Gathering the Desert, Gary Paul Nabhan, Paul Mirocha (Illustrator), Univ. Arizona Press.

Ocean Power: Poems from the Desert, Ofelia Zepeda, Univ. Arizona Press.

Of Earth and Little Rain: The Papago Indians, Bernard L. Fontana, John P. Schaefer (Photographer), Univ. Arizona Press.

O'Odham Creation and Related Events, (The Southwest Center Series) as told to Ruth Benedict, Univ. Arizona Press.

Papago Woman, Ruth Murray Underhill, Waveland Press.

Rainhouse & Ocean: Speeches for the Papago Year, Ruth Murray Underhill, Donald M. Bahr, Baptisto Lopez, Jose Pancho, Univ. Arizona Press.

Singing for Power: The Song Magic of the Papago Indians of Southern Arizona, Ruth Murray Underhill, Univ. Arizona Press.

The Desert Smells Like Rain: A Naturalist in Papago Indian

Country, Gary Paul Nabhan, North Point Press.

The Geography of Childhood: Why Children Need Wild Places, Gary Paul Nabhan, Stephen A. Trimble, Beacon Press.

Additional Materials for Teachers

The Tohono O'Odham, Jacqueline D. Greene, Franklin Watts/ Grolier Publishing.

Myths & Legends of the Indians of the Southwest, Bertha Dutton & Caroline Olin, Bellerophon Books.

Southwestern Indian Arts & Crafts, Mark Bahti, K C Publications, Inc.

Southwestern Indian Ceremonials, Tom Bahti, K C Publications, Inc.

Southwestern Indian Tribes, Tom Bahti, K C Publications, Inc.

The Papago Indians and their Basketry, Terry DeWald, author/ publisher.

Source Materials for Students

Animal Energies, Gary Buffalo Horn Man, Dancing Otter Publishing.

Gathering the Desert, Gary Paul Nabhan, Paul Mirocha (Illustrator), Univ. Arizona Press.

Ocean Power: Poems from the Desert, Ofelia Zepeda, Univ. Arizona Press.

Of Earth and Little Rain: The Papago Indians, Bernard L. Fontana, John P. Schaefer (Photographer), Univ. Arizona Press.

The Tohono O'Odham, Jacqueline D. Greene, Franklin Watts/ Grolier Publishing.

Southwestern Indian Arts & Crafts, Mark Bahti, K C

Publications, Inc.

Southwestern Indian Ceremonials, Tom Bahti, K C Publications, Inc.

Southwestern Indian Tribes, Tom Bahti, K C Publications, Inc.

The Papago Indians and their Basketry, Terry DeWald, author/ publisher.